A WAYWARD MISS

A WAYWARD MISS

Gillian Kaye

CHIVERS

THORNDIKE

This Large Print edition is published by BBC Audiobooks Ltd, Bath, England and by Thorndike Press®, Waterville, Maine, USA.

Published in 2004 in the U.K. by arrangement with Robert Hale, Ltd.

Published in 2004 in the U.S. by arrangement with Robert Hale, Ltd.

U.K. Hardcover   ISBN 0–7540–6969–9 (Chivers Large Print)
U.K. Softcover   ISBN 0–7540–6970–2 (Camden Large Print)
U.S. Softcover   ISBN 0–7862–6608–2 (Nightingale)

The text of this Large Print edition is unabridged.
Other aspects of the book may vary from the original edition.

Set in 16 pt. New Times Roman.

Printed in Great Britain on acid-free paper.

British Library Cataloguing in Publication Data available

Library of Congress Control Number: 2004103121

For Liz

CHAPTER ONE

Anthea felt that she must get out of the house. Her grandfather lay dead in his large, bare bedroom upstairs; his son, who was her Uncle George, had not yet arrived and the lawyer was not expected until the afternoon.

Loxley Hall was a tall, narrow building of brick, built at the beginning of the eighteenth century and it had been Anthea's home for five-and-twenty years. She had come to it when she was two years old and had no memory of her arrival. She had never liked the house, remembering the cold stone floors and the threadbare carpets of her childhood, the dark heavy furniture and the shabby curtains. The only thing that had made it a tolerable place was the presence of Grandmama Haley who had made the little orphaned Anthea welcome and had brought her up with a love in her heart which was entirely lacking in her husband, Anthea's grandfather, Sir George Haley Bt.

But outside the Hall it was different. The faithful Enoch Peel had tended the gardens all his life and here was the one place that Anthea could feel any comfort or sense of beauty. The Hall stood on high ground not far from Lanercost Priory in Cumberland and from the steps of the small gazebo at the end of the garden, Anthea loved to look towards Hadrian's Wall. There she could lose herself in imagination to a time when life was even more rigorous than it was in 1815 . . .

'Miss Anthea.'

Anthea turned just as she had reached the gazebo to see a breathless Mrs Drewery hurrying towards her. Mrs Drewery was Sir George's cook and the only friend Anthea had at Loxley Hall.

'Mrs Drewery, you have been running. What is it?' Anthea asked with some concern, for the good woman was short and heavy and not young. 'Come and sit down in the gazebo. Why didn't you send Polly for me if you wanted to see me?'

Mrs Drewery sat down and fought to regain her breath. 'Had to tell you myself, Miss Anthea. Mr George—oh, I suppose I should say Sir George now—has arrived before time and not in a good temper. Straight away he was put out because you was not there, started shouting at me to go and find you, so I guessed where you was and came running as fast as I could.'

'What has put my uncle out of temper?' asked Anthea.

'I think he's afraid Sir George has left his money and the Hall to you.'

Anthea stared. 'But why should he think that? He is the heir. I am hoping Grandpapa will have made some provision for me, but it is

2

Uncle George who inherits.'

'But you know they had that quarrel when Lady Alice died and they hasn't spoken since.'

'Mrs Drewery,' Anthea spoke decisively as she remembered the past, 'you know as well as I do that my grandfather cut my mother out of his will when she married the curate of Mayfield who was my dear father. She died when I was born so I have no memory of her and although I was only two years old when my father died, I like to think that I have this feeling of love and kindness which can only have come from him. And then—'

Mrs Drewery interrupted with a smile. 'And then you came to Loxley Hall and your grandfather wasn't going to have it, but Lady Alice over-ruled her husband for once. I can remember her very words, listening at the door I were though I shouldn't have been. "Anthea is our granddaughter and her place is here. You cut out your own daughter when she married Edmund and we lost her. The same thing is not going to happen to Anthea, George, and I will have my way in this." That's what she said and I've told you so many times.'

Anthea smiled. 'She was wonderfully kind, wasn't she?'

'Yes, she was, and she brought you up like the daughter she had lost. God rest her soul and now the master gone, too. Twelve years have slipped past since she left us, Miss Anthea, and you sticking to your grandfather

3

all that time and running around as though you was his paid housekeeper just to save him the money. An old skinflint he was, though I shouldn't be speaking ill of the dead.'

But Anthea had to agree. 'There is no denying he was a skinflint, Mrs Drewery. The years it took me to get those dreadful shabby curtains in the drawing-room repaired and a few rugs to make the entrance look less bare.'

'Well, I hope he's left you nicely settled, that's all. I can say that even if he had to leave the Hall to his son.'

Anthea was curious. 'Has my uncle changed, Mrs Drewery? Don't forget that it's also twelve years since we saw him last.'

'He's got fat and I expect that wife of his is fat, too.'

'Mrs Drewery, you are being disrespectful.'

'I'm sorry, Miss Anthea, but you remember as well as I do the scene we had when your poor grandmama died.'

Anthea did remember. She had been fifteen at the time, a rather plain young girl, grief-stricken at the loss of the person who had been as a mother to her.

After the funeral, she had sat in the library with her uncle and her Aunt Augusta and an angry grandfather.

'Father,' the Hon. George Haley had begun, 'you are going to be on your own now and I must tell you that Augusta and I think that it is quite ridiculous for you to live in Loxley Hall by yourself. It will be mine eventually and it would suit us, with our growing family, to move into the Hall straight away. Our Leeds house is barely big enough for us.'

Sir George Haley had eyed his eldest son and heir. The two had never dealt well together and the older man had become very curmudgeonly after his favourite daughter, Jane, had disgraced the family by running away and marrying a local curate. 'George,' he had said and he had spoken very stiffly, 'your mother was buried today, but I'll have you know that it is not my time yet. When that time comes, and not before, the Hall will be yours, unless I change my will and leave it to Anthea. It is her home after all.'

Then had followed what Anthea had thought of as an unholy row, her uncle and her grandfather both shouting abuse at each other and her Aunt Augusta screaming and crying and adding to the dreadful scene. It had ended with the younger Haleys ordering their carriage and leaving within the hour. Not a word had been spoken between father and son since that time.

'You are thinking of it, Miss Anthea.' Mrs Drewery's voice broke into her thoughts.

'Yes, it was shameful and I can only think that Uncle George is afraid that his father changed his will in my favour. I suppose I had better come in and see him.'

Mrs Drewery got up. 'Yes, I think you had. I

expect you'll be able to handle him now.'

Anthea laughed. 'I don't know about that, Mrs Drewery, but I can try.'

Anthea Davenport was a commanding figure as she walked at the side of the plump, little Mrs Drewery on her way back to the Hall.

She was now seven-and-twenty and considered herself, after an unhappy love affair, to be on the shelf. Anthea was handsome rather than pretty, but some, when seeing her dark eyes flash with humour and her strongly shaped mouth curve in a smile, would have described her as beautiful.

She never dressed fashionably for her grandfather had not given her an allowance and she herself made what dresses and gowns she needed from the lengths of material she bought from the market in nearby Carlisle. Even these items and the few ribbons purchased to decorate a bonnet had to be regarded as part of the housekeeping money.

But because of her height and her splendidly straight carriage, because of her glorious brown hair with its hint of red she made an arresting figure with an attraction and a beauty of which she was completely unaware.

Entering into the hall of the big house, she bumped straight into her Uncle George. And she was almost knocked over in spite of her height, for here was a man of immense proportions. She had to look up a long way to meet his now angry gaze and she soon saw that when Mrs Drewery had called him fat, she had not exaggerated. His great girth bulged from tight buff breeches and his bright red waistcoat laced with gold seemed absurd. Each button strained to keep it fastened across his broad chest.

'Anthea . . . good God, you've grown. How do you manage to be as tall as that? My sister Jane was a little thing. I suppose it must have been that disgraceful fellow of a parson she ran off with.'

Anthea eyed him in dislike. 'Uncle George, you are being insulting about my parents. I didn't ever know them but I hold them in respect.' Their eyes clashed and she could see a worried look in pale-blue eyes that seemed out of place in such a large and fleshy face. 'I suppose you have come to hear the will read. The funeral is tomorrow.'

'Of course I have and it had better be in my favour. You have had the run of the place all these years and it is time for me to have my proper inheritance.'

'You express no regret at your father's death?'

'I feel no regret. He did nothing to oblige me when I needed it most. And I've no doubt he treated you as a servant, his own granddaughter.'

Anthea had never felt any affection for her

7

grandfather for he had been forever out of patience with her, but she suddenly felt that she must rush to his defence.

'He was very sad after my grandmother died, but he has given me a home all this time.'

George Haley glared. 'Well, as far as I am concerned, it will not be your home for very much longer.'

Anthea did not reply and quickly ran up the stairs to her bedroom fearful that she might lose her temper with her uncle. She sat on her bed and thought of the events of the past few days.

Johnston, her grandfather's valet, coming to her at the breakfast-table to tell her that Sir George had died in his sleep; then, no sense of sorrow but rather a worry about what she should do with the money she was sure her grandfather would have provided for her. She knew that Loxley Hall would pass to her Uncle George.

Then the rush to get into Carlisle to send a letter on the mail coach to tell her uncle of his father's death. There were no other family members as far she knew. Her grandparents had produced two other children besides George and Jane; one a boy who had died at birth, and the other a girl who had been killed in a riding accident when only twelve years old.

So, Anthea was, saying to herself, there is only Uncle George and myself to inherit Grandpapa's wealth. For she knew that Sir

George Haley had been a wealthy man; the Loxley Hall estate was a valuable one and he had inherited fortunes from both sides of his family. At least I won't have to worry about money, she thought, it is deciding where to set myself up that will be the biggest problem. I could buy a property in Carlisle and find myself a companion, I suppose; it is unlikely that I shall marry now. Not after losing Christopher, her heart told her, and she swiftly put all thoughts of her former love from her mind.

Anthea and her uncle partook of a nuncheon without saying a word to one another and shortly afterwards, she heard the sound of the lawyer's chaise being driven up to the front door.

She knew and liked Mr Keighley. He had been kind to her after the death of her grandmother and on subsequent visits when Sir George had business deals to settle, the lawyer had been both polite and pleasant.

They sat in the library. A dark room with small windows and ancient curtains which Anthea had never been able to persuade her grandfather to change. It was a library in name only as there were few books; the baronet had not been a bookish man.

Mr Keighley sat behind the desk and had laid his documents neatly in front of him. Anthea thought he looked worried and not his usual amiable and placid self. Surely my grandfather has not left his estate away from his son, she said to herself?

She and her Uncle George were the only other people present and both sat rather stiffly in upright chairs in front of the desk.

Mr Keighley made the usual preamble to the reading of a will then gave a slight cough as he fingered the document in front of him.

'This is the last will and testament of me, George Henry Aloysius Haley . . .'

Anthea seemed to hear no more until the lawyer came to the words ' . . . my son George Arthur Carruthers Haley.'

She waited in vain to hear her own name then saw Mr Keighley lay the piece of paper down in front of him and look at her. There was no mistaking the fact that in his eyes was an expression of sorrow and pity. She became aware that her Uncle George had jumped up.

'That's it. Well done. I must go and order the carriage and get back to Leeds to tell Augusta the good news.' He shook hands with Mr Keighley, did not spare Anthea even a glance and walked from the room.

She tried to call after him. 'But the funeral, Uncle George . . .' But he was gone.

In the silent room, Anthea sat rigid and still with disbelief. Her name not mentioned? Nothing for her?

Then she saw Mr Keighley rise from his chair and come round the desk to sit at her side; he was a tall, scholarly looking man with white hair and he laid a hand gently but firmly on her shoulder.

'I am so sorry, Miss Davenport, but I could never get him to change it.'

Anthea came out of her daze and tried to speak. 'Does it mean there is nothing for me?'

The lawyer sat in the chair recently vacated by George Haley. 'I'm afraid not. You may not have noticed the date of the will, but it was made the day after your mother married Edmund Davenport. When you were made an orphan and came to live at Loxley Hall, I tried to get Sir George to make provision for you and I mentioned it several times since then. But he was absolutely unforgiving and he was adamant.'

'But he had quarrelled with Uncle George and I have kept house for him all these years; I thought at the least he would give me a pension. Does it mean I am penniless?'

'I am afraid so, my dear, unless you have any savings of your own.'

Anthea spoke as from a great distance. 'I have nothing; he did not even give me an allowance. And my father was in debt when he died though I believe it was settled. I can hardly believe it, Mr Keighley: what shall I do? I am not even allowed to stay at the Hall according to Uncle George.'

'They are hard people, the Haleys. You are not like them, Miss Davenport, you take after your mother and grandmother, don't you?'

11

She nodded. 'Yes, I suppose I do . . . Mr Keighley, I shall have to think. I could always get a post as a governess, couldn't I? I will have to try and make a living in the world.'

Edward Keighley looked at the girl sitting so straight in her chair and trying her best to hide her distress. He had a great admiration for Anthea Davenport and he asked his next question quietly and carefully.

'You are not thinking of marriage, Miss Davenport?'

Anthea's thoughts swept back over the years to the time when she had thought she would marry Christopher Stewart who was the youngest son of their nearest neighbour. It had all gone wrong and her heart had never mended. No, she was not thinking of marriage, but she had to make a civil reply to the kindly lawyer.

'No, I do not have marriage in mind, Mr Keighley.'

'Not to Mr Ambrose Stewart of Brampton Lodge?' he asked with some hesitation.

She stared at him. He looked serious enough but she felt scandalized, for Ambrose Stewart was Christopher's father. 'Mr Stewart?' How she managed to keep her voice steady she did not know for she felt angry. 'Mr Stewart is old enough to be my father. I know very well that he has been a widower for many years, but why do you think it would be a possibility? I fail to understand you.'

Mr Keighley looked grave. 'I can only be honest with you, Miss Davenport. The last time I mentioned to Sir George that he should make some provision for you, he seemed to think that you would marry Mr Stewart.'

Ambrose Stewart was not only a near neighbour, he had been her grandfather's only friend. 'They must have talked about it between them,' she said. 'I must tell you, Mr Keighley, that I would scrub floors rather than marry Mr Ambrose Stewart.'

'You have a reason, Miss Davenport? It would be an advantageous match for you. I know that Mr Stewart is your senior but he owns a fine house and estate and is a respected figure in the neighbourhood. I don't think that you should dismiss the idea too lightly.'

Anthea stood up then and faced Mr Keighley solemnly. 'I will never marry Ambrose Stewart and I do not wish to hear his name mentioned again. I will ask you instead if you know of anyone in need of a governess?'

Mr Keighley stood, too, and looked at the proud face. He would have to be brutally honest with her, but at the back of his mind he had an idea that gave him hope.

'Miss Davenport, a governess is expected to have received some education before she is entrusted with the young members of any family. I am afraid that your education was sadly neglected by Sir George; he did not even supply you with a governess.'

Anthea knew it was true and began to feel desperate. 'It is true, Mr Keighley, all I know is what I have read from the books in this poor library. And they are mostly the classics of the last century though I do have the works of Shakespeare given to me by my dear grandmama—but I run on, if I am not suited to be a governess what can I do? The only thing I know how to do well is to run a big house. I have had the ordering of Loxley Hall for the past twelve years.'

'You would be prepared to be a housekeeper in a big house, Miss Davenport?'

She met his eyes and saw that he was serious. 'I've never thought about it; if I can manage Loxley Hall then I suppose I should be able to manage any other house, but how do I go about finding a place? Is there an agency for such things?'

Anthea asked the question with a glimmer of hope, perhaps all was not lost. Then she heard Mr Keighley's next words.

'Miss Davenport, I know nothing of such agencies, though I know there are places for securing maid-servants. What I have in mind is something quite different and I must warn you that the idea is very tentative. I am reminded of a letter my wife received yesterday from her cousin who lives near York. The two of them have been more like sisters and have corresponded ever since Polly married and went to live in Yorkshire.' He stopped speaking and gave a short laugh. 'And such letters! All the local gossip and written in a very small hand and crossed. I don't know how they ever make them out, I'm sure—but I am sorry, I must get to the point. Polly happened to mention that there is excitement in the village as Felbeck Abbey, the biggest house in the district, has a new owner. The old Earl of Felbeck has died and his son, just back from Waterloo, has taken the place over. He is not married and has pensioned off the old earl's housekeeper and is looking for someone else . . .' He broke off. 'It seems too much of a coincidence that you should need such a position just at this time. Would you like me to write to the earl and put your name forward? I can assure you that a letter from me would be a recommendation in itself'

He said this in all modesty but Anthea felt she could have hugged him. 'Mr Keighley, you are a dear gentleman and a very good friend. I would be very pleased if you could write to your wife's cousin. I had not thought of going into Yorkshire but I do not see why not. I have nothing to keep me here and will be better off at a distance from my Uncle George.'

The lawyer took his leave assuring of his best attention and efforts on her behalf. 'I must see your uncle, Miss Davenport. I need his signature on several documents and he must not be allowed to leave before his own father's funeral.'

Anthea showed him to the door herself and not knowing where the new owner of Loxley Hall was to be found and also wanting to avoid him as long as possible, she went upstairs to her bedroom.

She had a very small room, but she considered it to be the most comfortable in the house. She had made rugs for the floor and had cut down curtains from one of the unused downstairs rooms to fit the small windows. She had made space for a small table and a chair from the dining-room, but when she wanted to be more at ease, she always sat on her bed. She had piled it high with cushions, they were soft and bright with the covers that she herself had embroidered with coloured wools.

She had a lot to think about that day, a lot of plans for the future but she found herself drawn into a past that was still vivid in her memory.

She was sixteen years old and still mourning the loss of her grandmama; she was learning the running of the big house and growing confident. Her greatest joy was to go riding and every day, wet or fine, found her out and about the estate and the surrounding hills on Shula, her beloved mare.

It was on one of these rides that she had met Christopher Stewart for the first time; she knew of him because of his father's visits to see her grandfather, but they had never met before as she was not considered old enough

16

to go to any routs or parties, indeed she received no invitations.

She and Christopher struck a chord with each other straight away. He was a handsome boy with dark hair and blue eyes and was a year older than Anthea. After that first meeting they rode together almost every day and he taught her to fish in the nearby Loxley Beck. One year went by and Anthea knew that she had fallen in love with Christopher Stewart; another year and she expected a betrothal to be announced for Christopher had kissed her more than once and had sworn his love for her. Yet another year and there was still no announcement, but Anthea was only twenty and she was happy; she had not made a come-out into local society but this did not worry her as she had no suitable dresses or gowns and she had Christopher.

Then came the day that was etched in her memory as though it was yesterday yet she found it hard to realize that it was seven years ago. That day, she had been standing by the beck holding Shula's reins and waiting for Christopher to arrive. When he did come and jumped off his horse with his usual light bound, she could see that he was not smiling but looked serious and somewhat anxious.

'What is it, Christopher?' she asked straight away as he came up to her.

He did not waste words. 'This is goodbye, Anthea.'

She stared in perplexity. 'What do you mean?'

'We have to say goodbye; my father is sending me into Scotland to marry my cousin. She has just come into a property and is considered quite wealthy.'

Anthea's face was ashen white. 'But, Christopher, what about us?'

He shrugged his shoulders. 'I'm sorry, Anthea, it has been lovely all these years. But I am a younger son and you are just your grandfather's housekeeper. I must do as my father says and marry well. He has it all arranged. I am going tomorrow.'

Anthea didn't cry, she lost her temper and she never remembered losing her temper before. 'You said you loved me, you even gave me kisses; I thought we would marry one day. And now you are to marry a wealthy heiress and all you can do is come to say goodbye? I hate you, Christopher Stewart; go and do what your father bids you and I hope your cousin is an ugly shrew!'

He said nothing. He looked at her with contempt, jumped on his horse and rode off. She had never seen him since. But she had thought of him, thought of her love, thought of her wicked words at their parting and regretted them many times.

And still she regretted them after all this time and now she had to think of what Mr Keighley had said. Marry Ambrose Stewart?

18

Marry Christopher's father, the very man who had torn her love from her grasp?

She would not think of it. She would think more of the promise that lay in the letter of Mrs Keighley's cousin from Yorkshire. It was a remote chance, but it gave her a tiny shred of hope on what seemed a very black day.

She did not dwell on the unkind act on the part of her grandfather. He had loved his daughter, Jane, and had never forgiven her for betraying the family pride of the Haleys. I will put all these years to good purpose, Anthea finally said to herself, I may not have any money but I have all the skills of running a big house economically and I must put these skills to some advantage.

Sir George Haley was buried next day in the village churchyard and Anthea found herself sitting in the small church with her Uncle George. She was conscious that the imposing figure of Ambrose Stewart was sitting behind them. Mr Keighley was the only other mourner and she found his presence a comfort.

Back at Loxley Hall, the new baronet was closeted with the lawyer for an hour before driving off to his wife and family and Anthea found that she had to be polite to Ambrose Stewart.

He reminded her of her uncle for he was large and portly and this did not endear her to him. That day, he was dressed all in black

19

except for a plain grey waistcoat and starched white neck-cloth. He was not a fashionable man but he used a good tailor.

Anthea found him gross and fawning at the same time. She disliked him not only because of her past grudge against him but for his over-familiar manner.

Anthea,' he addressed himself to her, 'I am afraid that your grandfather's death has left you alone in the world except for George and his family and he will soon be taking up residence at Loxley Hall. I know it has long been his wish to be here and as he is now Sir George Haley, he will lose no time in settling his affairs and moving his family here.'

Anthea thought there was no need for a reply. They were in the drawing-room and she stood staring out of the window, her eyes registering for the first time that the trees were showing their first signs of autumn for it was now late September.

Then she stiffened as she felt a hand on her shoulder; the big man had moved to stand behind her without a sound. As the plump hand moved caressingly over the smooth black of her mourning-dress, she felt the shock of revulsion and turned swiftly to face him. He did not give her time for words but pulled her close to him and silenced her protest with a kiss.

She stared at him powerless and listened to his words with a growing sense of horror.

'There, my dear Anthea, I've wanted to do that for a long time, but I was prevented all the time your grandfather was alive for he needed you. But I made a promise to him that I would marry you and give you a home at Brampton Grange. And now the time has come to claim you. Anthea, I am asking you to marry me and come to the Grange as my wife; we need not delay as I have obtained a licence and I long to make you mine . . .'

His hand went again to her shoulder and neck and Anthea stepped back quickly for she could not bear his touch. She struck out at him and felt the sting of her hand against his cheek; then she walked to the door leaving him gaping in astonishment.

'I will never marry you, Mr Stewart. I loathe you. My grandfather has left me destitute because of your expectations. I am making arrangements to go and live in Yorkshire.'

And she rushed from the room only to be confonted by her uncle. 'I'm off, Anthea, everything signed and sealed and I hope to be back with Augusta and the children within a sennight, so I hope you have settled things with Stewart. Augusta will be pleased to have you as a neighbour . . .'

'Uncle George,' Anthea's voice was icy. 'I am not going to marry Mr Stewart and I will be sure that I am not here when you bring your family. You can tell my Aunt Augusta that she will find the house in good order if somewhat

21

shabby, the servants are excellent. Goodbye.'

And she left him and shut herself in the library where she knew she would find Mr Keighley.

She went up to the lawyer who was still sitting at the desk; as she reached him, he rose and took her hands.

'You have received a proposal from Mr Stewart, Miss Davenport?' he asked in a gentle manner.

Anthea smiled then. 'Oh, Mr Keighley, I have been so rude to both Mr Stewart and my uncle. I don't know what has got into me, it is not like me to be so ungracious. But I find Uncle George infuriating and Mr Stewart repulsive. I long to be away from here.'

'I understand, my dear, and we must hope for good news from York. A letter has been sent off with the London Post Coach this morning so I think we can hope for a reply within the week. I promise to keep you informed.'

'You are very good, Mr Keighley; I feel as though you are my only friend.'

'Sir George behaved disgracefully towards you and I must do my best. I will be on my way now and will return with news as soon as I have it.'

CHAPTER TWO

The visitors departed, the house seemed very quiet and Anthea repaired to the kitchen for she knew that Mrs Drewery would be anxious for news.

The little woman dusted flour from her hands and drew up a chair at the big scrubbed, wooden table for Anthea.

'Oh, Miss Anthea, that worried I've been after you telling me that Sir George had left you destitute; I wouldn't have believed he could be that wicked.'

Anthea sat down. 'To be fair to him, Mrs Drewery, I don't think he meant to be wicked. He thought I would marry Mr Stewart.'

Mrs Drewery looked askance but she placed the kettle on the hob before saying anything. 'Marry Mr Stewart and him old enough to be your father, I never heard of such a thing, I'm sure. But I suppose it might do, for you would be mistress of Brampton Grange and able to hold your head up in local society. Has he made you an offer then, Miss Anthea? Have you accepted? Oh my goodness, I can't believe it though I suppose it might answer.'

Anthea laughed then. It seemed a long time since she had laughed but this was her very own dear Mrs Drewery. Her grandfather had treated them as equals, housekeeper and cook, the only difference being that as cook, Mrs Drewery had been paid a wage.

'No, Mrs Drewery, I did not accept him. I'm afraid I was very rude to him, but he is not a gentleman I hold in any esteem and he did not behave properly either.'

'Not behave . . . he never tried to kiss you and you in mourning?'

This made Anthea laugh even more and Mrs Drewery made tea and they talked over all the events of the last few days. When Anthea told of the plan to go as a housekeeper, Mrs Drewery was scandalized.

'But, Miss Anthea, you are a lady. Oh, I know you've acted as unpaid housekeeper to Sir George all these years, but that's different from going to an earl's house as his paid servant.'

'I'd rather be the paid servant to the Earl of Felbeck than be wed to Mr Ambrose Stewart. You might call it the lesser of two evils, but I think I would like to be in Yorkshire though I would miss you, Mrs Drewery.'

'I suppose Mr George will keep me on though he might bring his own cook and servants with him from Leeds.'

'We'll have to wait and see. I think you will find my Aunt Augusta a reasonable woman. I remember her as being quiet and placid if somewhat ruled by her husband. But she is devoted to her children—don't forget they were married late and their children are young, but she will bring her own nursery-maid with her. I think it will be rather nice to think of Loxley Hall being opened up again and all the rooms used and to hear the sound of the children.'

'You are right, Miss Anthea, you always were one for looking for the best in things and I'm sure I wish you well if you go off to Yorkshire even if I don't approve of you doing it.'

For the next few days, Anthea felt restless but occupied herself by making a decent dress from a bolt of rust-coloured sarsenet which had lain in the attics since her grandmother's day. She had determined to herself that if she were to obtain the post with the Earl of Felbeck then she would go out of mourning. No one there would know that she was so recently bereaved and she felt too young to spend the next year in black.

She did not receive the expected visit from Mr Keighley but he sent her a message with his clerk.

Dear Miss Davenport
I am very sorry that business matters have kept me from coming to see you, but I wanted you to know straight away that I have received an encouraging reply from Yorkshire. Would you kindly attend my office on Monday next to meet Mr Stephen Lorimer, steward to the Earl of Felbeck. I

look forward to seeing you.
Edward Keighley

Anthea read the note with a stir of excitement and felt pleased that she had almost finished work on her new gown; if anyone in Carlisle should see her out of mourning dress, it just could not be helped, she told herself.

For all the late Sir George's mean ways, he had always kept a carriage and if Rob Coachman was elderly, he was kindly and held Anthea in some respect.

She was driven into Carlisle on the following Monday in good time for her appointment and felt composed and confident knowing that she looked well in her new gown. She wore it with a pelisse of dark brown and a bonnet which failed to hide the rich colour of her hair.

At Mr Keighley's offices, she was shown into the room by his clerk and thought for a moment that she must have interrupted a visit from another of the lawyer's clients.

Mr Keighley was standing by the window talking to a tall, slim gentleman whom she thought looked not much older than herself. She later discovered that he was indeed nine-and-twenty. He was dressed in what she considered to be the height of fashion though she admitted that she was no judge. He wore breeches of the palest grey under a coat of blue superfine which was a perfect fit for his slim build; his waistcoat was modest and also grey and his starched neckcloth neatly folded. That he was handsome there was no doubt; his mouth fine and well-set, his eyes blue and keen and his hair which was very fair, brushed forward in a Brutus style.

Anthea dragged her eyes away from him and listened to Mr Keighley.

'Miss Davenport, may I introduce Mr Stephen Lorimer, steward to the Earl of Felbeck. Mr Lorimer, this is Miss Anthea Davenport of Loxley Hall who I think for the purpose we have in mind we will address as Mrs Davenport.'

Stephen Lorimer stepped forward, gave a formal bow and touched Anthea's hand. She felt slightly bewildered as she had expected a much older man and certainly not a man dressed as though he was about to make a morning call.

His first words echoed her own thoughts about himself. 'You are younger than I had expected, Mrs Davenport,' he said as they sat down in front of the lawyer's desk. 'But I believe you have considerable experience of the management of a big house.'

Their eyes met and Anthea felt a stir of liking together with an odd feeling that her future was to be linked with this good looking young man.

Mr Keighley let them talk together without

27

interruption and, at the end of half an hour, the matter was settled. Anthea, styling herself Mrs Davenport, would travel to Yorkshire in a week's time to become the housekeeper at Felbeck Abbey near York. Mr Lorimer said he would look forward to renewing her acquaintance and working with her at Felbeck; his blue eyes were telling her that he admired her.

Mr Keighley saw her out of the room and before they had reached the outside door, he had observed that something was worrying his client.

'Very satisfactory, Miss Davenport, I am pleased that we have been able to arrange it for you and wish you success. But I can see something bothers you, is there anything I can do to assist you?'

Anthea looked up at him. She felt uncomfortable, but he was the only person she could turn to. 'Oh, Mr Keighley, I have no money. I should be booking my place on the London Post Coach while I am here in Carlisle and I really need to purchase some material to make myself a suitable dress for travelling. What shall I do?'

'Do not worry.' His eyes twinkled. 'We can arrange these things without anyone being the wiser. I have the handling of the late Sir George's affairs and I will give you a sum to cover your needs which I can put down to my expenses. Do you think twenty guineas would

28

be enough?'

She gasped. 'Oh, that is much more than I shall need, Mr Keighley.'

'I think you deserve more, for Sir George played a shabby trick on you after all the years you devoted yourself to him. Sit there and I will go and see my cashier and give you the money in guineas, I think that is the most practical way. And you can run off to the milliners and buy some ribbons to trim your bonnet; we can't have you looking the dowd!'

Anthea smiled her thanks. 'I have never met anyone as kind as you, Mr Keighley. I will write and tell you how I fare at Felbeck Abbey. It sounds very grand, doesn't it?'

'You will do well, I am sure of it, and I will look forward to hearing all about it and so will Mrs Keighley. Goodbye, Miss Davenport and God speed.'

A week later, Rob Coachman had to take the carriage into Carlisle before the sun was up as the London Post Coach left the town at five o'clock in the morning.

Anthea was seen off from Loxley Hall by a tearful Mrs Drewery who was certain she would never see her mistress again. Anthea kissed her and promised she would return once a year if she could.

A guard helped her into the coach where she felt embarrassed to find herself to be the only lady travelling. However, the other passengers were all men of business and very polite and helpful to her. Out of Cumberland they were soon in Yorkshire, but she found they still had a long way to go before they would reach York. The windows of the coach were small but she had glimpses of wild moorland scenery before they reached the broad plain of York and approached the city by Micklegate Bar.

Anthea had never before seen anything like the narrow and crowded streets of York. In some places the old Tudor shops and buildings overhung the narrow street but they were soon turning into Coney Street and her destination, the Black Swan Hotel. The coach did not stop there for long before continuing its journey to London.

At the Black Swan, Mr Lorimer had told her that there would be a footman to meet her and escort her to the earl's carriage for the journey of four miles out of York to Felbeck Abbey.

Anthea was helped down from the coach and given her travelling bag. She found herself in a crowd of jostling travellers, for the Black Swan was one of the main posting-houses of the city.

'Mrs Davenport?'

She turned quickly. A short man of middle age was approaching her, he was dressed in dark-red livery and she guessed he was the earl's footman.

'Yes,' she nodded. 'Are you . . . ?'

'I'm James and His Lordship's carriage is waiting for you. Let me carry your bag.'

He was polite and helpful, handed her into the carriage and she was left to travel the short distance on her own while he sat beside the coachman.

Felbeck Abbey lay between the villages of Skelton and Shipton a few miles out of York on the road to Thirsk. With every passing moment, Anthea felt herself growing more and more apprehensive. But I will not show it, she kept saying to herself, and glanced out of the window at flat, rather uninspiring farmland, broken here and there by a house or cottage, perhaps a copse of trees.

She felt the swerve of the carriage as it turned into a long drive but she did not catch a glimpse of the house until she was helped from the carriage by James.

Then she looked in awe for she had not seen an Elizabethan manor house before; it was of mellow brick and the casement windows were large. There was a wing at each end of the building and the front door was protected by a large square porch. She was fascinated by the tall chimneys and thought she had never seen a more interesting house, or one which conveyed at first glance such an impression of solidity and grandeur.

James, still carrying her bag, opened the front door for her and Anthea saw straight away that there was no big entrance hall as at

31

Loxley. The entrance was rather a low-beamed room leading to a broad staircase which turned on a wide landing. He led her into a small room which seemed both dark and gloomy; thick velvet curtains were half drawn across the windows and it appeared to be barely furnished.

'Mrs Davenport, My Lord, I will take her bag up to her room.'

James's voice broke into her thoughts and looking across the room, she saw a man propped up on cushions, half-lying on a sofa. She could see that he was not an old man, but that was all. His dark hair was untidy, grey eyes glared at her, and his face was creased in a frown as though he was in some pain.

When he spoke, his tone was irritable. '*You* are Mrs Davenport?'

'Yes,' she replied quietly, not knowing whether to address him as 'My Lord' as James had done. Surely this could not be the Earl of Felbeck?

'Yes,' she said again, then she saw him give a wince of pain as he tried to sit up straighter to look at her. She found herself at a loss and spoke hastily. 'I am sorry, you are in some pain; were you injured at Waterloo or in the Peninsula?'

He grunted. 'Nothing so heroic—I was there, but have no thrilling tales to tell and I came back unscathed a month ago.' He shifted awkwardly. 'This happened yesterday trying

32

out a new horse of mine. I didn't know he had such vicious ways; he threw me at a hedge. It is nothing, except my back is damned painful; I will be up and about tomorrow.'

Anthea said the next words without even thinking whom she was addressing. 'My grandfather always used Webster's Liniment for such injuries. Would you like me to procure some for you?'

'And would you rub it in?' he rejoined, and was instantly ashamed for he saw her handsome face go red and her lips tighten in a straight line.

'You jest, My Lord.'

'And so do you, I think, ma'am. You are saying that you are the Mrs Davenport my steward has appointed as my new housekeeper? I'd better tell you that I am the Earl of Felbeck and I do not like to be thwarted.'

Their eyes met and clashed, grey against brown, and Anthea found herself preparing to fight. The earl was obviously in some discomfort and would have to be excused his tetchiness.

'I am Anthea Davenport—Mrs Davenport —and I was interviewed by Mr Lorimer at my lawyer's office in Carlisle. I made the arrangment with him to travel to York today, My Lord.' Anthea thought she sounded superior and she knew it would not suit the stricken man. It did not.

'I may not be able to get on to my damned

feet, but I can see at a glance that you are not suitable. You are too young and too beautiful. What was Stephen thinking of? Did you cast those dark eyes at him?'

Anthea stiffened; she had been pleased enough to secure the position as the earl's housekeeper, but she sensed that she could never like or tolerate the owner of Felbeck Abbey and she spoke out in her usual forthright fashion.

'I am neither young nor beautiful. I am seven-and-twenty; I have kept house for my grandfather for twelve years and my looks are only passable. I am sorry if you are in pain. Is there a sedative I can get for you, some laudanum perhaps?' But she seemed to say nothing that would please him.

'There is nothing I want, it's just this damned back of mine. I'll be up in the morning, have to be away for a few days. You'd better stay the night and be off back to wherever you came from tomorrow: there's no standing having a housekeeper younger than I am. Stephen must have had his reasons, you'd better send him to me.'

'My Lord . . .'

'Don't argue, woman, go and find Stephen and leave me in peace.'

Anthea turned away from the disagreeable man; there was no crossing him in this mood. She would find Mr Lorimer.

Outside the room, she found a narrow

34

passage that she thought might lead to the kitchen, from where she could hear sounds of laughter. A few seconds later, she was standing in the largest kitchen she had ever seen and found herself looking at a disgraceful scene.

At the wooden table at its centre sat a fat, red-faced woman and by her side was an elderly man with white hair and a face as brown as a berry as though he lived and worked out of doors. They were passing a bottle between them and from the smell and the fumes, Anthea knew that it was gin and that they had obviously drunk half the bottle already.

When they heard the sound of the door and looked up and saw her standing there, they gawped. Anthea could think of no other word.

'I am Mrs Davenport, the new housekeeper,' she said loudly.

'Lor',' said the woman and staggered to her feet. 'Out you go, Ned, better not have any more.'

The man grinned and disappeared from the kitchen by the door which seemed to lead into the back garden.

'I'm Mrs Cook, the bailey . . . er, I'm Mrs Bailey, the cook . . .'

'You are drunk, Mrs Bailey.'

'No, miss, not drunk, just a bit tipsy; me and Ned we always have a sip after dinner's served.' Anthea thought the woman's tone insolent and made up her mind to dismiss her in the morning. That is if there is going to be a morning, she thought grimly. What a start to her new life and expectations.

'You've had more than a sip, I think. Kindly tell me where I shall find Mr Lorimer.'

'Mr Lorimer? He'll be in his office the other side of the front door.'

'Thank you, Mrs Bailey, I'll see you in the morning. Is there a maid who will show me to my room?'

'Oh yes, miss; I'll send Sally straight away, she'm only out in the yard hanging out the drying cloths.' And the cook waddled to the back door and called out loudly, 'Sally, come 'ere quick. The new ma'am has come and wants her room.'

A very small girl came in looking very scared; she had fair curls under her cap and Anthea could see a fading bruise on her fore-head.

'Are you Sally?' she asked kindly, for she liked the look of the girl.

'Yes, m'm.'

'Please show me to my room.'

'And mind you be'ave,' shouted Mrs Bailey after her.

Anthea followed the little girl up the broad staircase and was shown a bedroom at the front of the house. She saw that her travelling bag had been placed on a stool under the window. She looked around; a large room, low-ceilinged and rather bare; no rugs and tattered curtains. What had she come to?

'This is the housekeeper's room, Sally?'

'Yes, m'm, they always have this room.'

'Always, Sally? Do you have a lot of housekeepers?'

'Yes, if you please, m'm, they won't stay, you see.'

Anthea knew it was wrong to gossip with a servant but she was more than curious.

'Why don't they stay?'

'It's the master.'

The earl? Anthea thought. What was going on here? 'Does the master hit you, Sally?'

Anthea asked the question with a sudden disquieting feeling, but Sally was quick to reply.

'Oh no, m'm, he's kind is the earl. It's Mrs Bailey, though she'd kill me if she heard me talking to you. Always at the bottle, she is, and whoever's housekeeper doesn't know what to do with her and the master sends them off. Now you've come, but I don't suppose you'll stay any longer than the others. It's a pity because I think you're nice and no one's ever spoke nice to me before.'

'Well, off you go, Sally, and don't tell Mrs Bailey that you've been talking to me. If she asks, say you've been helping to unpack my bag, that would be all right.'

Sally beamed a lovely smile and Anthea thought she was a pretty little thing. Then she took off her bonnet and pelisse, tidied her hair though there was no looking-glass in the room and decided to go and find Stephen Lorimer.

Downstairs there were several doors which might be his office and she tried the one nearest to the front door. To her astonishment, she found herself in a long, low room which she thought must be the drawing-room but which had every piece of furniture under holland covers.

As she came out, she found Mr Lorimer standing in the small entrance.

'Mrs Davenport, you have arrived. Were you looking for me? My office is here, do come in. That is the drawing-room, but it is never used as you can see.'

Thank heaven, she thought, as she followed him into his office, he is as good-looking and as pleasant as he was at Carlisle. Perhaps he will explain what is happening here.

'Mr Lorimer, I am very pleased to see you for I have questions to ask of you as you did not tell me the whole when we met in Carlisle.'

'Come and sit down and I will pour you a glass of wine. And have you eaten? I will arrange a supper for you.'

His room was plain but comfortable. There was a fire burning in the grate and two chairs on either side of it. She sat in one of them and he poured her a glass of wine and put it on a small table in front of her. Then he took the other chair.

'Have you met Marcus yet?' he asked her. 'I'm afraid he's not at his best for he took a tumble yesterday. Not like him at all for he can usually do anything with a horse, but he's bought this brute of a hunter. I knew it was a mistake as soon as I saw it, but Marcus insisted that it wouldn't get the better of him. Was wrong though, the beast unseated him at a hedge down at the Long Acre. He's put his back out but his man will rub some liniment in tonight and he'll be as right as rain in the morning. I expect you found him out of sorts.'

She had listened in silence and then decided she could speak her mind for he was both friendly and open. 'I did. In fact, he has told me that I can stay the night, but that I am to go back to Cumberland in the morning. He said he didn't know what you'd been thinking of to give me the position as I was much too young. So I thought I should come and ask you what I should do.'

'Don't do anything. Marcus will change his mind in the morning. He hates being laid up and out of action. I will have a word with him; you are not to worry.' He smiled at her and she felt her worries receding.

'That's not all,' she then said to him. 'I found my way to the kitchen and there was the cook sitting over a bottle of gin with the gardener. A pretty little servant girl showed me to my room and she had a bruise on her forehead. I had a word with her, Sally is her name, and she informed me that you have had a succession of housekeepers who cannot handle a drunken cook.'

Stephen Lorimer groaned. 'The truth will out. You see, we were desperate for a really strong character for a housekeeper, someone with experience. As soon as I saw you I knew you were the one. I looked at you in that lawyer's office and knew that you would be able to cope with Mrs Bailey. So I got you here. You will know what to do, won't you?'

She shook her head. 'It does not make sense, Mr Lorimer. If the earl has a drunken cook, why does he dismiss his housekeepers and not the cook? It's a nonsense.'

'I know it might seem like that, but she's a wonderful cook, you see, a genius. Marcus doesn't often entertain here. But if he does, even if she's been on the bottle, she produces the most tempting dinners. He's the envy of everyone around. But the housekeepers can't manage her so they go.'

'And I am to go before I even try to manage her?'

He shook his head. 'No, we'll see what happens in the morning. I promise you that it will be all right and that you will be able to stay. You needed this post, didn't you?' His expression was kindly.

'Yes, I did, and I've not come all this way just to turn round and go back again.' Anthea got up and he rose with her and held out his hand. Without thinking, she put hers into it and she liked the feel of his cool fingers. 'I will go back to my room—it needs furnishing, by the way—and perhaps you would arrange to have a supper sent up for me. I think I am better out of the earl's way for the rest of the evening.'

'Have you a fire in your room?'

'Yes, I think the little Sally must have seen to that. I must keep an eye on her.'

He pressed her fingers. 'I am glad you have come, ma'am. I think we are going to see changes for the better.'

Anthea went back to her room and a few minutes later, Sally appeared with a plate of cold meat and some crusty bread; there was also a tankard of ale but Anthea did not drink it.

She found the unwelcome-looking bed quite comfortable and slept well in spite of her forebodings about life at Felbeck Abbey.

Next morning, she went down the stairs in search of the breakfast-room, to find a tall figure in a travelling coat with several capes, regarding her sardonically as she took her last steps into the hall.

CHAPTER THREE

Anthea assumed that the earl must have a visitor when she saw the tall gentleman, then, as he turned to speak to her, she gave a gasp as

41

she heard his voice and realized that it was indeed the earl himself.

'Well, Mrs Davenport, I trust you are ready to make your journey back to Carlisle.'

He was looking down at her and there was steel in his gaze.

'You are recovered, My Lord?' was all she could say.

'Just a slight stiffness. My man Robert is a genius when it comes to injuries. He was with me right through the campaign in the Peninsula . . . but that is by the by. I have spoken to Stephen, but I will not be persuaded by his glib tongue; I need someone much older and with some authority. You are the fourth housekeeper to arrive at Felbeck Abbey in as many weeks and you are no more suitable than the others. I am pleased to make your acquaintance and wish you a good journey home; I have arranged for you to be taken into York. I will be away for a few days on business so I will bid you farewell.'

'My Lord . . .' Anthea was determined to put her own case.

'No, don't stop me, my carriage is waiting.' And without another word, he made a polite bow, turned and let himself out of the front door. A few seconds later, she heard the sound of the carriage wheels on the gravel as they started off down the drive.

What an unbearably rude man, she said to herself, why ever do I feel I want to stay here?

Is it the challenge? Is it because it seemed to be the only opening for me and I was glad to leave Loxley Hall behind? And what do I do now? She started to walk slowly up the stairs and with each step, a deep feeling of gloom and failure overcame her.

But before she had reached the half-landing, she turned to the sound of her name being called.

'Mrs Davenport . . . Anthea . . .'

She was glad to see Stephen Lorimer at the foot of the stairs but she thought his expression was anxious.

She hurried down to join him and without saying anything further, he took her by the arm and led her into his office where they sat facing each other across the fireplace.

'You did not succeed in persuading the earl to let me stay?' she asked uncertainly.

He shook his head. 'For some reason he has taken you in dislike and will only declare that you are too young. I have a feeling he thinks I may have appointed you for my own amusement.'

Anthea half rose. 'Mr Lorimer, what are you saying?'

'Sit down, please sit down and I will try and explain. When I came back from Carlisle, I was full of praise for you but I did not mention your age so Marcus was expecting a much older person. He didn't expect Mrs Davenport, the housekeeper of Loxley Hall for twelve

43

years, to be young and beautiful—'

Anthea stopped him. 'This is absurd, I am no beauty and never will be. In fact, I told the earl that for he made the same silly remark. My looks are not above the ordinary and well you know it.'

Stephen looked at her. She had some indefinable quality that indeed was not beauty; it was more the expression of confidence and ability that came from her dark eyes and was almost a radiance. Was it any wonder that Marcus had been suspicious, the steward thought? But now he somehow had to put matters to rights because he had not changed his initial opinion that Anthea Davenport would be just the housekeeper that Felbeck Abbey needed.

'Mrs Davenport, would you be prepared to listen to something I must tell you before we decide whether you make the journey back to Carlisle or not?'

She protested. 'But the earl told me he had arranged a carriage for me.'

'We can easily change those plans. Marcus is going to be away for a few days. Did he tell you?'

'Yes, he has just left.'

'Now I must tell you why he has gone and I can do so without betraying any confidences.' He looked at her seriously and she nodded her head but said nothing in reply.

'Marcus Lorimer, eighth Earl of Felbeck

inherited the Abbey when his father died several months ago. Marcus was in Spain at the time and the news of his father's death reached him too late for him to come home for the funeral. I was already home from France having received a slight injury so I came up for the funeral—Marcus is my first cousin, you know—and I was shocked to see how run down Felbeck Abbey had become. Half the rooms were shut up; you are already aware that the drawing-room still is, and there was a general air of neglect and shabbiness. There was no housekeeper and the place seemed to be ruled by the dreadful Mrs Bailey who cooked such splendid dinners! I hope I am not boring you, I wish you to know just what we are faced with.'

Anthea was in fact, gripped with interest; she had noticed how shabby everything appeared to be and had wondered about it. 'No, it's interesting, do carry on,' she replied.

'I think you know that there have been a succession of housekeepers none of whom stayed for more than a few days and you can see that a lot needs doing to restore Felbeck Abbey to its former glory. The first thing Marcus did when he returned from Waterloo was to send for me and ask if I would like to be his steward. I was delighted and my first task has been to try and secure a housekeeper. So far, I have failed miserably and all my hopes were on you when I returned from Carlisle. I think I must have kept silent about your age because I knew just what Marcus would say.'

'And he did.'

Stephen smiled. 'Yes, he did, and now he has gone away for a sennight I think it is our chance.'

She met his eyes in astonishment and she could see a keen eagerness in his expression. 'I do not understand you. The earl told me in no mean terms that he did not want me here.'

'I think we might practise a little deceit.'

'Whatever do you mean?' she asked quickly but her interest was captured.

He moved his chair nearer to hers. 'Let me tell you the rest of the story if you would kindly be prepared to listen. Marcus has gone away for a particular reason. You see, he has a young ward. Her name is Miss Jennette Goodison and she is coming to live here with a cousin of Marcus as her companion and chaperon—'

'Oh my goodness,' interrupted Anthea. 'Is she a young girl? The place is not fit to bring a young person into.'

'Exactly; you have grasped my meaning straight away.'

'Do you mean . . . ?'

He nodded. 'Yes, I do mean that you should stay here for the time Marcus is away and try and put the house to rights. It will not only make a more suitable homecoming for Jennette, it will establish you as a fit housekeeper in Marcus's eyes. We can then hope he will have no wish to send you away.'

Stephen Lorimer looked at Anthea and was not surprised to find her eyes dancing. I was not mistaken in her, he said to himself. 'Would you be willing to do it?'

She leaned forward and spoke eagerly. 'It is the kind of challenge I love. It will be a deceit as you say, but we have nothing to lose. I will transform the house and if the earl is still displeased with me then I will return to Carlisle, or seek another position in York.'

He took her hand in his and once again, she had a feeling of pleasure at his touch. 'You really will do it? You are a remarkable girl. I thought I might be able to appeal to you. Can I go and tell the coachman you will not be needing a carriage?'

She smiled, rescued her hand and stood up. 'Yes, I think you can. May I have your permission to start straight away? And may I ask you two things?'

'Yes, of course.'

'The first thing I intend to do is to dismiss the cook and I would like you to know that.'

Stephen looked at this unusual girl and wondered for the first time if he was doing the right thing.

'Dismiss Mrs Bailey? Oh, but Marcus—'

'The earl will soon get used to someone else cooking his dinners. I will find a local woman or, if necessary, I will do the cooking myself

47

until I find the right person. It would not be the first time I have had to cook a dinner for grand company.' Anthea felt as though her little world was somersaulting. One minute cast down and now here she was full of enthusiasm and confidence.

Stephen looked almost rueful. 'I trust I have made the right decision, Mrs Davenport. No, I am going to call you Anthea and you must call me Stephen if we are to work in this together.'

'I will see, Mr Lorimer.'

'And what was the second thing you wanted to ask me?' he said next.

'I would like to see the room that is intended for Miss Goodison. I think it is of the first importance to make it nice even before I put the drawing-room in order.'

Stephen walked with her to the door. 'I think I must leave it in your more than capable hands, but first I will take you upstairs and show you Jennette's room.'

The upstairs passages of Felbeck Abbey were gloomy but the steward opened the door of a large room with a window which faced over the extensive gardens and land at the back of the house.

Anthea noticed immediately that the furniture was dark and heavy and of a previous century and made up her mind to look around the house for something more suited to a young lady of quality. The hangings at the window and bed were dark and in some places worn into shreds. She wondered if something new could be made in the space of a week.

She nodded. 'It will do; it is low but spacious and the outlook is pleasant. I think I can make the necessary improvements.'

'You will ask me if there is anything you need?'

She turned and looked at him; he had lost his worried expression, but she had the feeling that he doubted her ability to make the necessary changes on her own. 'Mr Lorimer—no, I will not call you Stephen, it is not proper and it is too early in our acquaintance—I know what I want to do, but if I have any doubts or problems, I promise to come and tell you. Will that satisfy you? And first of all will you let me have five guineas please?'

He stared at her but did not demur. 'Five guineas? Yes, certainly, Mrs Davenport. I must tell you that it is my custom to ride round the farms in the early part of the day, but you will usually find me in my office before dinner.'

'Thank you, Mr Lorimer.' Anthea waited until he had fetched a bag of guineas from his office then went to her room. There she found a sheet of paper and wrote down all the changes she wanted to make. It was a long list.

My first task is to tackle Mrs Bailey, she said to herself, as she finished writing, and it is going to be the most difficult one.

Luck was on her side for although it was only ten o'clock in the morning, when she entered the kitchen, she found the cook slouched in a chair at the side of the stove with a gin bottle already between grimy fingers. There was no sign of Sally or any of the housemaids who, Anthea imagined, must be elsewhere in the house clearing the grates and lighting the fires.

'Mrs Bailey.' Anthea's voice was sharper than she had intended.

'Woz that? Oh, it's only you, miss; the master's away a few days.' Mrs Bailey didn't even move but raised the bottle to her lips and took a gulp.

'Mrs Bailey, I have come to dismiss you.' She was so disgusted at finding the cook already drunk at such an early hour that Anthea did not find her task as difficult as she had thought it would be. 'You are not fit to cook for anyone and certainly not in His Lordship's house. A drunken cook is a bad example to the other servants and I can see from looking around me that their duties have been sadly neglected. The stove needs blacking, the brass is in want of a good clean and polish and I can see scraps of rotting food on the floor.'

'It's that Sally . . .'

'No, it is not "that Sally". She is so scared that she does not dare come near you; don't think that I didn't see the bad bruise on her forehead.'

'I'll 'ave 'er—'

'No, you won't have her. Here is five guineas and it is more than you deserve. I want you packed and gone before noon, do you understand? And if you have a relative to go to, please leave the address and I will ask the earl to send a character reference. It is more than you should expect but I understand that your meals are something out of the ordinary.'

'You can't dismiss me, you only arrived yesterday and His Lordship would never hear of me going.'

'His Lordship has made me his housekeeper.' God forgive me for the lie, Anthea muttered to herself. 'And you will do just what I say. It is my word that counts and if I have any more arguments from you, I shall advise the earl not to give you a reference.'

These last words seemed to matter, for the slatternly woman got up from her chair and went round the kitchen gathering things that were obviously her own possessions; these included various pieces of grey-looking underwear which had been set out to dry.

'Don't know where you'll find some as can cook like me,' she grumbled. 'I'll be at me daughter's in Skelton. I'm going up to my room to fetch my belongings and then I'll get Ned to carry them into Skelton for me. And I'm sure I hope as you can't get no one.'

'Then I shall do the cooking myself,' said Anthea and stood over the woman as she climbed the narrow servants' stair to her bedroom. Half an hour later, Mrs Bailey and Ned were to be seen, both of them laden, trudging down the drive. The sight gave Anthea a good deal of satisfaction.

I've done it, she said to herself. Now I've got to find out what servants we have. And she went in search of James, the footman who had met her in York.

'Mrs Bailey gone?' he echoed, when Anthea told him what she had done. 'I never thought I'd live to see the day. And it's a good thing if you don't mind me saying so, miss. What do we do now?'

'Who waits at table when we have a formal dinner?'

'I do.' His Lordship does not have a butler or a serving-maid.'

Anthea was thoughtful. 'Gather the servants together, James, I'll speak to them and then I must go in search of a cook.'

Getting the servants together was a very easy matter for, to her horror, Anthea discovered that there was only Sally and a big capable girl who gloried in the name of Clarissa but said she was usually called Clarrie.

She set them to go round each room in the house and to clean thoroughly. 'Do as much as you can,' she told them. 'I want all the furniture shining and not a speck of dust anywhere. I am going out now to find a new cook and I will try and bring two extra maids back with me.' Then she went in search of

52

the steward.

She caught up with him in riding clothes and about to go out of the front door.

'Stephen . . .' she called without thinking, and he turned at the sound of her voice and burst out laughing. She started to feel annoyed but then realized what had occasioned his laughter.

He came towards her and smiled. 'You called me Stephen.'

'Yes,' she said ruefully. 'It seemed to come naturally and I suppose I can't be formal if we are to be in this plot together.'

'I'm glad you see it like that, Anthea, I promise not to take advantage. You wanted me for something?'

'Yes, Mrs Bailey has gone and Sally and Clarrie are cleaning through the house for me. I have to go in search of a cook and there is only one person I know in the area. She is the lady who told my lawyer's wife of the position at Felbeck Abbey in the first place and she lives in Shipton. Is it too far for me to walk, or do I have a horse or a conveyance at my disposal?'

I don't know if Marcus is going to like this, Stephen was saying to himself but it was my idea and I am committed to going along with it now.

'It is over a mile away,' he replied. 'We are slightly nearer to Skelton than to Shipton and I do not suggest that you try and walk that far.

Marcus has taken the carriage and Samuel Coachman, but there is the old gig in the stables. It hasn't been used in an age, but I think one of the stable boys will have kept it in good condition. We could easily fasten Derry to her. She's an old pony but very reliable and quite suitable for the rough lanes. I take it you are used to driving yourself?'

'Of course,' she said, then realized that she had spoken rather shortly. 'My grandfather allowed me to have my own phaeton in Cumberland, but of course, I must forget those days. I am a servant now.'

Anthea,' he grinned at her with a friendly smile. 'You are the most unlikely servant I have ever met and what Marcus is going to say to all this, I shudder to think.'

'We will see when he returns with Miss Goodison,' she said coolly.

Anthea knew only Mrs Keighley's cousin's name, Amy Tuke. But it was not difficult to find her in the small village of Shipton and she stopped at a modest but substantial stone cottage and knocked on the door. A maid answered and took her name and from the room behind, Anthea could hear the surprised voice of the lady who had been instrumental in bringing her to Yorkshire.

'Miss Davenport? My goodness gracious me, show her in, Lucy, and go and tell Miss Sarah to come . . . oh, and you had better bring some wine, too.'

Alice had expected Mrs Tuke to be little and round and comfortable, she did not know why for she found her to be quite the opposite. She was a slender grey-haired lady, dressed in grey and wearing a white cap. She showed open delight at Anthea's arrival at her cottage. 'Miss Davenport, well I never. I do hope as everything is all right at Felbeck Abbey for you. It's a lovely old house and I hope you will be comfortable there . . . oh, and here's my youngest, Sarah. This is Miss Davenport, Sarah, who has come from Cumberland to be housekeeper to His Lordship.'

Anthea found herself greeting a sensible-looking girl as tall as her mother and with very little to say.

The wine was brought in and Anthea took a small sip before she explained her mission.

'I've come to seek your help, Mrs Tuke. I will be quite honest with you and also trust you not to let this become local gossip. Felbeck Abbey is a lovely old house as you say and I think I will like it there, but I must tell you that I have dismissed the cook . . .'

Mrs Tuke did not allow her to continue. 'Dismissed Mrs Bailey? I don't believe it. She should have gone years ago with her drinking as she does; a scandal it's been though I know she is an excellent cook.'

'That is where I hope you will be able to help me, Mrs Tuke. Do you know of anyone who is a competent cook and who would come to the house for at least a few weeks until I have got the place in order and can go into an agency in York?'

Mrs Tuke fortunately took Anthea seriously. 'I really don't know, Miss Davenport, all the people I know are either suited already, or they are just young girls who want to go into service as maids like my Lucy . . . no, don't look so disappointed, let me think for a minute.'

There was a silence then Anthea heard the quiet but assured voice of Sarah. 'Couldn't I go, Mama?'

Her mother looked at her askance. 'You, Sarah? Oh, no. I know we are not gentry, but we Tukes can hold up our heads in society.'

'But, Mama, I am weary of being at home and I am not spoken for and you know I love to cook. You so often say that I would make someone a good cook.'

Anthea was listening with interest. Sarah seemed to be about four-and-twenty, not a pretty girl, but neither was she ill-looking, having both sense and intelligence in her eyes. Yes, it is interesting, Anthea said to herself.

'Would you like to try it for a few weeks, Sarah? I cannot promise you more than that as it would be a kind of trial period. You wouldn't mind leaving home and living at Felbeck Abbey?'

Sarah shook her head. 'No, I should have left home before, but the young man I was betrothed to was killed at Vitoria. I would like to try, Miss Davenport, if you would have me and my mother agrees.'

Mrs Tuke gave a sigh. 'I cannot disagree, can I? It is a good chance for Sarah and I want her to do well; she's always loved to cook since she was a little girl.'

Anthea smiled at them both. 'Is that settled then? And could you come tomorrow, Sarah? I will send a pony cart for you. And, Mrs Tuke, the young girls wanting positions as maids; could I ask you to choose two of the most suitable and send them along, too? As far as I can see, there are only two maids at Felbeck Abbey and there is a lot of work to be done. I also need a sewing-woman if you know of one, just for a week.'

It was all settled and the next day, Jed and the pony cart brought Sarah Tuke, together with Nancy Heywood and Rosie Kay to Felbeck Abbey.

Then began a week of feverish activity and Anthea enjoyed every minute of it. Sarah was horrified at the state of the kitchen and she and Sally set to and got it cleaned before any cooking was done. Only cold meat was served on that day.

Anthea went from room to room, discovering treasured pieces of furniture which had been neglected for years. She took curtains down and had them washed until they seemed to come up in a new fresh colour. And she got her new and willing servants to scrub and polish until they were tired out. Mrs Tuke had also sent the willing Mrs Scargill, an excellent needlewoman, who at once set to making and remaking curtains and hangings.

Then Anthea found the attics. They were no more than holes in the roof space approached by a few narrow wooden steps. And here were her greatest finds; bolts of satin, Persian rugs, old Tudor furniture which must have been part of the house when it was built. It was solid and square, but most of it was beautifully carved and when it had been polished, she refurnished the drawing-room with it.

When Stephen saw the drawing-room for the first time, he could not believe it. Anthea had just hung new curtains and was admiring them when he appeared in the doorway; she had been so busy she had caught only the occasional glimpse of him all the week.

'Anthea, what have you done?' There was amazement in his voice.

She turned in delight. 'Do you like it, Stephen? I have turned it back into an old Tudor room, the furniture was up in the attics.'

'But it looks so light and bright in spite of the dark wood.'

She smiled. 'It's the new curtains. And the windows have been cleaned and the wood is gleaming. I feel quite pleased with myself.'

Then Stephen Lorimer spoiled it. He put

both hands on her shoulders and bent and kissed her lightly on the lips.

Anthea stiffened and took a step back. 'Mr Lorimer, that was uncalled for.'

'I'm sorry, Anthea, I shouldn't have kissed you. Please forgive me, you looked so delighted and beautiful that it happened before I really thought of what I was doing. Please regard it as a thank-you kiss for all you are achieving. Don't think that I haven't noticed the incredible change in the house.'

As Anthea had to admit to herself that she had quite enjoyed the kiss, she could not be cross after this praise.

'I am glad you like the drawing-room, I have tried very hard with it. Now, tell me about the picture above the fireplace, Stephen, is it of the Lorimer family?'

The kiss forgotten, they stood together in front of the fireplace and looked at an oil painting in a heavy frame hanging above the mantelshelf. It was a family portrait of husband and wife sitting in chairs with their children standing around them, with the exception of a small child dressed in cream lace and sitting on its mother's knee.

Stephen was nodding in answer to her question. 'Yes, it is the fourth earl and his wife, Catherine. It was painted by Van Dyck and I believe the occasion was the baptism of their youngest child. I think it is a very valuable painting though it is not as large as some of the Van Dycks painted at the time—he was court painter to Charles I, you know. It is much valued in the family.' He looked at the tall girl at his side. 'I do believe you have managed to clean the frame; it has always looked rather dull and grimy.'

'Yes, I did it myself. I had a feeling it might be valuable and didn't entrust it to one of the maids. It is very interesting. My own family is an old one, but we do not go back as far as that.' She started to walk across the room. 'Now I would like you to see Miss Goodison's room and ask you if you approve; I'm rather proud of it myself.'

They walked upstairs to the large bedroom which had looked so dark and uninviting when Anthea had first seen it. It was transformed.

Light velvet curtains hung at the windows and round the bed; the more elegant pieces of Georgian furniture had been moved from other rooms and the whole effect was both dainty and feminine.

Stephen smiled at her. 'I musn't kiss you again, must I?'

'No, certainly not,' she managed a laugh. 'Do you like the room?'

'It is splendid and I think you are very clever; how ever did you manage to get the curtains and hangings made in the time?' he asked.

'I didn't, I've had a sewing-woman here all the week, she has done wonders. And then I

60

had a piece of good fortune. I found a hoard of curtains and rugs and furniture up in the attics. We moved it all down, it wasn't really clever at all.' Anthea felt pleased with herself nevertheless but one doubt remained. 'What do you suppose the earl will make of it all?'

'I can't see that he can be anything but pleased unless he comes home a bit touchy about having to bring Jennette here. He's never been one for the petticoats though he must marry one day if the line is to continue.'

She looked at him. 'Perhaps he will marry his ward.' She said it rather as a joke, but he took her seriously and shook his head.

'I don't think so somehow, she is only eighteen years of age and he is more than thirty. It is rather a big age gap, is it not?'

'Maybe he will fall in love with her and the age difference will not matter!'

He laughed. 'You are being frivolous all of a sudden, my serious Mrs Davenport, I think your success with the house has gone to your head. By the by, you have had some success with your new cook, too. She has served some splendid dinners and seems to know what she is about when Jed takes her into York for meat and fish.'

Anthea was thoughtful. 'Yes, I am very pleased with her, but do you think I should expect fireworks when the earl discovers that Mrs Bailey is missing?'

'We shall see, I expect him back tomorrow

at the latest.'

'You make me feel anxious; do you think my days are numbered?' she asked him.

'Marcus is a very fair person. If he thinks you are competent, I don't suppose he will hold your age against you. And I will plead your cause, as well.'

'Thank you, Stephen. We might as well make a tour of the house now we are upstairs.'

Exactly twenty-four hours later with Anthea busy seeing to her own room, the last in the house to be made comfortable, she heard the sound of the carriage at the front and then voices coming from the hall.

The earl is back, she said to herself, and she felt her heart sink. I shall soon know my fate, was her sober thought.

In the small entrance hall, with its oak panelling now shining, stood four people.

The Earl of Felbeck still wearing his caped travelling coat but bare-headed, was looking around him slightly puzzled. Stephen was standing by his side and with him was a short girl looking a picture of enchanting prettiness. Golden curls peeped from her high bonnet, she had bright blue eyes and what Anthea thought must be one of the loveliest young faces she had ever seen.

Standing behind her and only just inside the door, was a small wisp of a woman of uncertain age and dressed in drab, her expression both anxious and awed.

At that moment, the expression on the face of Miss Jennette Goodison—for the pretty girl was indeed the earl's ward—was of pleasure and expectation as she looked up at her guardian.

But the earl was not looking at Jennette. He was watching Anthea, graceful and composed in a simple dress of deep red, walking slowly down the stairs.

'What the deuce are you still doing here? I thought I ordered you to leave?' His voice was both angry and impatient.

CHAPTER FOUR

Anthea paused on the stairs quite calmly and it was Stephen who spoke to his cousin. 'Marcus, I must tell you—'

'You need tell me nothing, something is going on between the two of you. I might have guessed it.'

Anthea had by now reached the bottom of the stairs and decided to ignore the irate manner of the earl and to greet his ward who was looking from one to another with a puzzled frown.

'You must be Miss Goodison,' Anthea said. 'Welcome to Felbeck Abbey. I hope you will be happy and comfortable here. I am Mrs Davenport, the housekeeper, and I trust you will come to me if there is anything you need. Please come into the drawing-room and I will—'

'No, not the drawing-room, it is not fit.' It was the outraged voice of the earl.

'Please come into the drawing-room, Miss Goodison,' repeated Anthea and opened the door. She knew her destiny lay in the next few moments and she was risking all by ignoring the earl's rising temper.

'Oh, what a lovely room.' The words came from Miss Goodison as she turned to her guardian. 'Marcus, I thought you told me that the house was a shabby place, but this is beautiful. I do love to see the old furniture. It reminds me of my grandfather's house.'

Anthea was watching the Earl of Felbeck and how she stopped herself from laughing, she did not know. His anger turned to bewilderment as he saw the refurbished room, then an appreciative satisfaction crept into his expression to be replaced in its turn by indignation as he turned to Anthea.

'Mrs Davenport, have you any explanation?' he asked stiffly.

She met his eyes proudly and did not give way. 'Oh yes, My Lord, I did not think you would want to bring Miss Goodison to a shabby house so I stayed on and made a few changes.'

She thought His Lordship was going to explode, but he was stopped by the calm voice of Stephen. 'Anthea has worked very hard, Marcus, let me show you round.'

The earl turned to his steward. 'Anthea is it? I was not mistaken. I will come and see what has been done.' He looked at Miss Goodison, then at the little woman who was hovering at her side and lastly at Anthea. 'I will see you in the library after dinner, Mrs Davenport. In the meantime, kindly take Jennette to her room, which I assume has been prepared and at the same time, find a room for Miss Craddock. This is Martha Craddock who has kindly come to act as chaperon to Jennette.'

He followed Stephen out of the room leaving Anthea with Miss Goodison, who was wandering round the room looking at various things, and with Miss Craddock, who suddenly found her voice.

'Mrs Davenport, I must say it is a surprise to find you here for Marcus told me he had been unable to get a suitable house-keeper. But you have made the drawing-room look so beautiful. It is just as I remember it when I was a little girl and I was used to visit my grandparents. My grandfather was the sixth earl, you know, Marcus is a second cousin, but I am pleased to be able to help him out. And Jennette is such a sweet child—Jennette, don't touch the pieces of porcelain, just look at them if you wish—and I am sure it will be a pleasure for me to live at Felbeck Abbey and not a bit of a duty. Marcus has even insisted on a salary

65

for me which I am sure was not necessary even though I am forever purse-pinched and relying on my sister for a home, until now that is . . .'

Anthea looked at the little woman in dismay. She is not as old as I first thought, she said to herself, she must be close on forty years. Is this how I shall become if I live to be an old maid? Depending on people's charity, talking about nothing at all—never, she vowed, I would rather remain the housekeeper at Felbeck Abbey for the rest of my life.

Then she turned towards the younger girl who had taken off her bonnet and was standing at the fireplace looking up at the family portrait.

'Mrs Davenport, is it Marcus's family hundreds of years ago?' she asked.

Anthea stood beside her unable to stop giving a little chuckle. 'Not quite hundreds of years, Miss Goodison. I think the portrait was painted in about 1640, it is the fourth earl and his family.'

Brilliant blue eyes were turned to her and they were brimming with laughter and mischief. 'My governess never could teach me my history,' she said. 'And, Mrs Davenport, I would rather you called me Jennette. Miss Goodison sounds so cold, and formal.'

Anthea smiled. This was a girl who could break hearts, she thought. It is not just that she is so pretty with those blue eyes and golden curls, she has an air of fragility about her. The earl and Stephen Lorimer are sure to want to protect her. She was soon to learn that far from being fragile, Jennette had a strong character and a wilful spirit especially when she wanted her own way.

But all she said was. 'Come upstairs and I will show you your room, I hope you will like it.'

The September morning sunshine was filtering through shining windows when they entered Jennette's bedroom and the young girl gave a gasp of delight. 'This is all for me? Oh how lovely. You have made it so pretty with those hangings round the bed. I have been living with my aunt while Papa was fighting in the war and I had to share a room with my young cousin. She was the untidiest little girl I have ever met.' She looked out of the window and sighed. 'It is lovely here, do you think Marcus will let me ride? I am used to riding out each day, you know.'

'I am sure he will find a suitable mount for you. Your trunk is here, Jennette; I will send up a maid to unpack it for you. Her name is Nancy and I think you will like her.' Anthea turned to Miss Craddock who had been standing uncertainly in the doorway. 'Miss Craddock, I will give you the room next to Jennette's, it is small but comfortable. I was not expecting you so the fire has not been lit yet, but I will send up the housemaid to see to it straight away.'

'It is most kind, Mrs Davenport, I am not used to such attentions though I do like to have a room of my own.' They stood in the room next to Jennette's. 'Oh, it is very nice and looks over the back of the house just as Jennette's does. My sister's house was in the town and I must say that I prefer to look out over countryside and I expect there will be country walks that I will be able to take with Jennette . . . oh, and there is even a small desk, that is very thoughtful for I will be forever writing to my sister to tell her how fortunate I am. And there is my bag already carried up for me but I can unpack it myself, you know, I don't have the need of a servant for I am very independent . . .'

'I will leave you to your unpacking then, Miss Craddock.'

'Thank you, Mrs Davenport, and I must . . .'

But Anthea had escaped. How ever will I tolerate her going on in such a fashion, she asked herself as she went down the stairs. Then she gave a chuckle at the wicked thought that perhaps she could leave the earl to put up with Miss Craddock's endless chat.

She visited the kitchen and found Sarah returned from York and all ready to prepare a dinner that would impress the earl. The girl had settled very well at Felbeck Hall during that week and Anthea was pleased with her; maybe she would not impress as Mrs Bailey had done, but she knew how to plan a dinner and exactly what she needed to buy in the way of fish and meat.

'Mrs Davenport,' Sarah said with some excitement as Anthea entered the kitchen, 'I am going to do my very best today. I purchased brill which I think is a good plain fish and I shall serve it with a shrimp sauce. Then I have an entree of veal cutlets and for the second course, I shall serve rump of beef from our own farm. Then there is grouse or partridge for the third course but I haven't quite decided on that yet. I have already made a *compote* of peaches and a plum tart and I am thinking of doing a blancmange as well. What do you think of that? I feel it is a special occasion with the earl returning with Miss Goodison and I must make a good impression. After today, we will be back to plain family dinners except when the earl is entertaining.'

Anthea was pleased and said so. 'It sounds more than satisfactory, Sarah. I hope that Sally is proving to be a good help to you.'

'She is a very willing little girl; she works hard and is always pleasant. I couldn't ask for better.'

Leaving the kitchen, Anthea found Stephen lying in wait for her at the door of his office. 'Anthea, I must speak to you for it is not good news. Marcus is very impressed with the house but he holds something against you. And he doesn't yet know of Mrs Bailey's departure. I am of the opinion that it will be all up with us

69

by this evening.'

But Anthea had confidence in Sarah and hoped the outcome would be better than Stephen was predicting.

'Leave it to me, Stephen,' she said, but she did not lift the look of gloom from his face until she spoke her next words. 'And what do you think of Miss Goodison? Is she not a very pretty girl?'

'Pretty?' he echoed, with a smile of pleasure. 'That is doing it too brown, Anthea. She is the loveliest little thing I have ever seen. We have been looking at a mare for her, she is a very keen rider which will please Marcus.'

'I am glad to hear that something will please him for he seems to me to be a most disagreeble man.'

'No, you don't know him, Anthea. It is true that something is upsetting him today; I think his Cousin Martha irritates him. Is she not a gabble-monger? You can walk away from her in mid-sentence and she doesn't even notice!'

'Yes, I know,' Anthea had to agree. 'But I think she has a kind heart and Miss Goodison needs a chaperon after all.'

Stephen gave a short laugh. 'I've a strong feeling that Jennette will soon be able to twist Miss Craddock round her little finger. They have already had one set-to as to whether Jennette is to be allowed to ride on her own or whether she must take a maid.'

'Oh dear, Miss Goodison should not ride on

her own, but I must admit it is very irksome to be accompanied everywhere just when you feel it would be nice to have a good gallop across the moor.'

Stephen looked at the handsome young woman. 'You used to ride on your own in Cumberland!' he said accusingly.

Anthea was remembering how she had soon shaken off the servant provided for her and had come to meet with Christopher. Then had followed the stolen trysts . . . but she shook her head, she must not dwell in the past. 'I'm afraid I did. I suppose I was rather headstrong in those days.'

Stephen laughed in delight. 'I think you are still headstrong now, my Anthea, and I think I know of someone else who is going to turn out to be headstrong or wilful, whichever you like.'

'You mean Miss Goodison?'

'Yes, she had very strong ideas on which mare would suit her and would not be fobbed off with Nellie who she thought to be a very poor creature. Jennette has settled on Tessa.'

'Tessa?' Anthea was remembering a high-spirited mare who would take a lot of handling. 'But she is too strong for Miss Goodison.'

'Not according to Jennette, she likes a horse to have spirit.'

'Oh dear, do you think we are heading for trouble?' She looked at him but he was smiling.

'Yes, there might be trouble but it will be interesting.'

They parted on good terms and with a laugh. Anthea went away hoping she could stay at Felbeck Abbey; she liked Stephen Lorimer.

As usual, Anthea ate her dinner in her room on her own. She could have joined Sarah and the maids in the kitchen but she felt she owed it to her position to have her meals served separately. Especially so as she had furnished the housekeeper's room downstairs very comfortably with a small dining-table and a chair as well as the desk at which she sat to do the household accounts.

She enjoyed her meal that night but could not stop herself from wondering how the company in the dining-room had fared. She was soon to find out.

A tap on the door brought Rosie with a message from the earl; Rosie had been promoted to serving-maid and was doing very well under James's guidance.

'Please, Mrs Davenport, His Lordship says would you join him in the library?'

Anthea rose and steadied her nerves. 'Thank you, Rosie,' she said quietly. When the girl had gone, she glanced in her looking-glass and saw to her satisfaction that her hair was neatly piled on the top of her head and that the stiff cotton dress of dark green with a small sprig of cream flowers in its pattern, was not

72

only suitable but that she looked well in it.

At the library door, she met Stephen coming out but he was not smiling and she feared the worst.

'Try and win him over, Anthea,' he whispered and disappeared in the direction of his office.

Marcus Lorimer, 8th Earl of Felbeck, had arrived back at his home with his ward and her companion and had felt an immediate annoyance that the young woman he had dismissed and thought he had sent back to Cumberland was still in the house. Then he had discovered the miracle she had made of the drawing-room and when Stephen had shown him the changes that had been made throughout the big, old house, he had begun to wonder if he should change his mind about Anthea Davenport. He had his own reasons for not wanting her as his housekeeper but he was trying to keep them hidden for he thought them both unreasonable and irrational.

Now, having partaken of one of Mrs Bailey's excellent dinners, he had to make a decision about Mrs Davenport.

When she tapped on the door and entered the library, he was struck again by her dignity and beauty. This was a woman fit to be a countess and here he was having to consider whether to employ her as his housekeeper. His feelings tugged at him to keep her; his common sense told him he could not have her

73

as one of his servants.

'Come in, Mrs Davenport, and sit down. Can I offer you a glass of port?'

'No, thank you, My Lord.' Her voice was cool and composed and he immediately sensed a battle.

'I must tell you that it is good to be home again and, especially to Mrs Bailey's cooking. That was an excellent dinner; indeed it seemed to me that she surpassed her best efforts. The beef was delicious.'

Anthea knew her hour had come. Stay cool, she said to herself. 'I have dismissed Mrs Bailey, My Lord.'

She met eyes grey with shock and consternation. 'Would you mind saying that again?'

'I dismissed Mrs Bailey on my first day here, she was both drunk and very insolent.'

He got to his feet and regarded her in a thunderous rage. 'Are you telling me that on the very day I asked you to leave, you had the audacity not only to stay on in the house but to dismiss the cook the family has valued for years?'

Anthea stayed sitting and looked up at him. 'Yes, that is correct. I discussed it with Mr Lorimer and as I could see that there was a lot wrong in the running of the house, we decided that I should stay for the time being. I was of the opinion that the cook's drunkenness was the reason for you not being able to keep a

74

housekeeper.' He did not say anything but looked at her malevolently and she continued calmly, 'The kitchen was filthy, the kitchen-maid had bruises on her face where Mrs Bailey had struck her, and the rest of the house needed a good clean.'

'So what did you do about this state of affairs without my permission or even my knowledge?' His tone was knife-edged.

'I sent Mrs Bailey packing, went out and found a new cook and took on two more maids. We have spent the whole week cleaning the house—including the drawing-room—putting up new curtains which I have had made and moving furniture. You must have noticed the difference.'

He glared at her harshly even though he could feel nothing but admiration not only for her action but also for her composure.

'You are the most infuriating woman it has ever been my misfortune to meet,' he said cuttingly. 'I dismiss you and you choose to stay. You get rid of the best cook in the district and you calmly admit that you have taken on extra servants and cleaned the house so that it is looking as it has not looked for as long as I can remember . . .' He found he was almost speechless for around her mouth played a little smile.

'You like what I have done in the house then?' she asked him and did her best not to sound self-satisfied.

'Of course I like it, the place is beautiful, what do you expect me to say?' He paused as though he had suddenly thought of something. 'And the library and my study? You dared to disturb them? What have you done to make it all look so different?'

'I moved nothing,' she replied and was speaking honestly. 'I did not think that proper in the rooms that were your own. They have simply been cleaned. Each book dusted, curtains washed and rehung and furniture polished. That is all.'

'Be damned to your efficiency, and what do I do now? I brought you in here determined I would not keep you as my housekeeper and you sit there as cool as a cucumber and give a recital of what you have done.'

Still she did not move and he reached down, took her by the arms and pulled her to her feet so that she was standing very close to him and looking into his eyes. She felt breathless.

'Why do you think I dismissed you in the first place?' He asked the question almost bitterly. 'I told you to go for precisely the reason I made at the time. You are too young and too beautiful and I did not want the temptation of you in my house—'

'My Lord,' Anthea interrupted, hotly and hastily.

'I did not want the temptation of your dark beauty,' he continued, as though she had not spoken, 'because it is my intention to marry my ward when she becomes of age. We are not formally betrothed for she is young and has yet to make her come-out. But it was a promise made to her father on his death bed and I intend to keep it.'

Even as he was speaking, he was drawing her nearer to him and she found herself powerless.

'I took one look at you, Mrs Davenport, and found you tempted me beyond belief because I am not known to be a ladies' man. I was lying helpless at the time, but the following morning as I was about to depart and saw you coming down the stairs, all I wanted to do was this . . .'

And saying no more, he pulled her into his arms and his lips sought hers in a demanding and passionate kiss.

Anthea had never been kissed in such a way before. Christopher's salutes had been chaste and brotherly in comparison—and instead of pulling herself away and recoiling in disgust, she found herself involuntarily pressing forward and returning his passion.

Suddenly she was thrust from his hold and would have fallen if he had not caught hold of her arms, his fingers hurting her with the tightness of his grasp. His eyes were angry and his words scathing. 'You see what I mean, Mrs Davenport? You see why I don't want you here?'

'I will go and pack my things instantly,' she replied.

'No, you will not, damn you. You have done wonders with this house of mine and I will not let you go. You have got it running smoothly; you have secured the services of an excellent cook, God knows how, and you have made my ward welcome. So what you will do next is to cease to be my temptress and become Mrs Davenport, my housekeeper. You will leave me to pay court to my ward, who sang your praises all through dinner I might have you know. And if you can, you will keep my dreadful cousin out of my way. I always knew her to be a silly woman and a chatterbox, but I have never heard anyone run on quite so much all about nothing!'

Anthea laughed then and sat down again. She was recovering from the overturn of her feelings at his kiss and she knew that she wanted to leave neither Felbeck Abbey or its owner. If his presence was a danger to her, she would bury her sentiments deep and concentrate on the smooth running of the house. And she had to remember that she had Stephen as a friend.

The earl sat beside her and took her hand in his. 'I have to apologize, don't I? I should not have kissed you and I have not behaved as a gentleman. Will you forgive me, ma'am?'

She nodded and withdrew her hand from his grasp. 'I must, My Lord, if I am to keep my position and I have to admit that I would like to stay.'

'Let us determine to be friends. We need not be as master and servant for I have discovered that your grandfather was Sir George Haley of Loxley Hall. Is that correct? If it is then it means that you are a lady and I am at a loss to understand why you have had to apply for this position at all.'

She told him of her circumstances and in a short while, the passionate and awkward moments forgotten, they found themselves talking comfortably together.

Anthea asked him about Felbeck Abbey. 'I would very much like to know why the house is called abbey,' she said to him. 'Does it mean that there was an abbey here at one time?'

He smiled, took her hand and pulled her to her feet. He must have sensed her reluctance for he gave a chuckle. 'Do not fear, Mrs Davenport, I am not going to kiss you again even if I am still tempted to do so; you are safe with me. I must ask you if you have not yet walked in the grounds? Let us have an evening stroll and I will tell you the history of the family and show you what remains of the original abbey.'

'But it will soon be dark, My Lord.'

'It is a pleasant September evening and I would like to take the air with you. As you are now officially my housekeeper, it is quite proper for me to show you round.'

It was indeed a fact that Anthea had been so busy she had not even stepped outside the doors of Felbeck Abbey since the day she had driven into Shipton and secured Sarah's services.

Now, as she walked at the earl's side past flower borders with fast-fading colours, she had the odd feeling that they were equals. They walked through a small orchard and Anthea found herself surrounded by low stone walls, scattered stones of a local grey and even a complete archway.

'This was the abbey,' she said with surprise and pleasure.

He looked down at her and liked what he saw. Her expression had lost the stiff defensiveness of having to justify her staying in his house as the housekeeper and her strong handsome features were relaxed in a smile. Here was not a pretty little thing like his ward but a woman of character and forcefulness who possessed the only kind of beauty that appealed to him.

'Come and sit down on these stones,' he said. 'I used to bring my books here when I was younger, the place had a feeling of solitude and learning that seemed to call me.'

Anthea listened to his words with some astonishment; he was proving to be a man of complex and surprising attributes and she wondered what she was going to discover next. He was certainly not the bad-tempered, self-opinionated person she had first thought him to be.

'I suppose the old abbey was pulled down in the time of Henry VIII,' she said.

'Yes, that is correct. Then Hugh Lorimer was of service to Queen Elizabeth and was created Earl of Felbeck in 1581. He proceeded to build the house which is still the family home to this day.' Marcus knew that he wasn't boring her, she was genuinely interested and showed it by her next remark.

'I am surprised that they did not build the new house with the stone from the abbey,' she said, looking around her.

He gave a laugh. 'By that time, all the stone had been carted off to build cottages in Skelton and Shipton.'

She nodded. 'Yes, I noticed when I went to Shipton that a lot of the cottages were built of stone.' Her remark was unthinking.

'You have been to Shipton? How was that?' he asked in some surprise.

She had to confess how she had come by Sarah and it brought them back to the affairs of the house.

'So she is a young person,' he said with a smile. 'I was quite deceived, but she is an excellent cook. I had put up with Mrs Bailey's habits because of her good dinners, but I can see now that you went about things in the right way.'

'Thank you, My Lord.'

'Do you have to call me "My Lord"?'

In the gathering dusk, she sought his

expression and found him to be quite serious. 'What else am I to call you? That is your correct title.'

'You could try Marcus.'

Anthea was immediately on her guard. 'Don't be absurd. Of course I cannot call you by your name, it would not be proper.'

'But it would please me; I would like to hear my name on your lips.' Anthea started to rise from their seat on the stones but his hand restrained her. 'Have I gone too far, Mrs Davenport?'

'I think you have, My Lord.' Anthea felt a sudden sense of intimacy between them, as though they could say anything they liked to each other. But she knew she must keep her distance. They had gone from being foes to being friends far too rapidly and she felt a growing feeling of closeness in their acquaintance which she must banish.

She was glad to hear him take on a matter-of-fact tone with his next words. 'Yes, Mrs Davenport, I will talk about more serious things. Is there anything more you would like to learn about Felbeck Abbey?'

'Not about the abbey,' she replied readily, 'but about its occupants. Would you mind telling me about Miss Goodison so that I know her exact position in the house and family.'

He stared across the ruins of his beloved abbey suddenly transported in time—and only a matter of months, he thought sadly—since the bloody scene above La Saint Haye at the battle of Waterloo.

At his silence, Anthea looked at him and saw his determined mouth straighten in a sad, grim line.

They were still sitting down and without thinking, she put a hand on his and he covered it instantly with his own as though glad of the comforting gesture. 'What is it, My Lord? Have I said something to upset you? It was not my intention.'

His hand still on hers, he spoke quietly. 'It is all right, dear girl, my thoughts were in the past and they are not happy ones.'

'Do you want to tell me?'

'I think I do, I have spoken of it to no one.' He looked at her serious, sensible face. Why do I feel I can unburden myself to a girl I have only known two minutes and who is my housekeeper, he asked himself, but was unable to answer his own question. 'Can you prepare yourself for a long story?'

'Of course,' she murmured and felt his hand tighten.

'I met Charles Goodison at Talavera. We were both cavalry officers and went through the Peninsula together; Almeida, Albuera, Cuidad Rodrigo, we saw them all and survived. Then came Waterloo and La Saint Haye; so many thousands went on all sides and Charles went, too, the best friend I ever had. He managed to ask me before he died if I would

83

be guardian to his only child, a daughter born to him when he was young man, eighteen years before. His wife had died long since and Jennette had been placed with cousins while Charles was in the Peninsula. But he wanted me to have charge of her; he wanted me to marry her and I promised him. As he took his last breath, I promised him.'

The earl got up then and walked away and Anthea knew compassion for him. As he turned back to her, she rose and put out her hands to him in an instinctive gesture and she was glad to see that he managed a wry smile.

'Why on earth is it I can talk to you? Why can I tell you things I would admit to no one?' He shook his head. 'I must tell you that I do not love Jennette, but she is a taking little thing and I think we might do well together. What do you think, Anthea?'

She noticed that he had used her name without even thinking, but she ignored it and felt she could be only honest in her reply. 'I've only known Miss Goodison for half a day, and I am sure that she is a very pleasant and well-behaved young lady.' She hesitated. 'I find it hard to imagine her as the next Countess of Felbeck. Is that being uncharitable?' she added.

He laughed and seemed to cast off his grim memories. 'I don't think it is in you to be uncharitable though I must say I think that you would have made the better countess.'

'Now you are talking balderdash,' she expostulated.

'It's not balderdash to me. You seem to have something exceptional about you. I can sense it after only a short acquaintance. I think if I was not promised to Jennette then I would be thinking about asking you to do me the honour of becoming my wife.'

'My Lord, please remember it is your housekeeper you are talking to. I should not be out here with you at all let alone be listening to such romantic nonsense. Let us become serious again for I wish to enquire about the previous countess, your mother; and your father, the seventh earl. How long is it since you inherited? I am sorry if it seems inquisitive but I feel it would make my position easier if I knew about the family.'

'It is not difficult, Mrs Davenport; my mother died when I was a small child. She was giving birth to the boy who would have been my brother.' Then his face clouded. 'I lived at Felbeck Abbey with my father and I had a tutor whom I loved and respected but who has since died. I went up to Oxford and then amused myself between London and York until the trouble came with Bonaparte and I went off to the Peninsula. I was at Toulouse when the news of my father's death reached me; Stephen had already gone home injured so I put him in charge of Felbeck and saw my time out with the duke. I had been home less than two months when you arrived and found me desperately trying to put the place in order; it had been very neglected in the last years of my father's life. You have achieved more in a week than I did in all that time. I suppose I must thank you.'

Anthea gave a light-hearted grin. 'Does it go against the grain to have to thank a mere housekeeper, My Lord?' But she had gone too far and had provoked him into familiarity.

His finger went under her chin and lifted her face to his; their gaze in the dim light was long and searching but she did not let her eyes drop. She had never before met a man like this. Her male acquaintances had numbered only Christopher and his father, and Mr Keighley, the lawyer. She found herself not sure how to respond to the earl's advances but it was not in her to shy away.

Then she heard laughter in his voice. 'I think a mere housekeeper might indulge in a little flirtation, Mrs Davenport,' he quipped, and for the second time in but an hour, his lips were on hers. This time they were light and caressing; they played with her, snatching little kisses that teased her and had the effect of making her yearn for the passion of the previous occasion.

At last she pulled away and forced normality into her words. 'It is getting dark, My Lord, I think we should return to the house.'

'I think you are right, Mrs Davenport,' he replied with an air of mock gravity in his voice. 'My ward will be wondering where I am.'

CHAPTER FIVE

When they reached the house, the earl went into his study which was a small room next to the library. Anthea thought perhaps she should go in search of Jennette to make sure that the young girl had everything she needed to make her comfortable.

Jennette was not in her room and Anthea was not sure where to look next but made her way to the drawing-room thinking that perhaps Jennette and Miss Craddock were sitting there waiting for the tea to be brought in.

She did not find Jennette but almost bumped into Stephen as she came out of the room.

He steadied her and smiled. He looked both pleased and in a teasing mood; she was getting to know his expressions. He was as handsome as ever and carefully dressed in white pantaloons for the evening and a nicely cut coat of dark grey.

It suddenly occurred to her that with his blue eyes and fair hair, he and Jennette would make a pair, but then she dismissed the silly, idle thought as it was obvious that the earl was pledged to make Jennette his wife.

'Anthea, I have been looking for you. Where have you been?'

'The earl has been showing me the ruins of the old abbey, it was very interesting.'

'You've been out of the house with Marcus? I do believe I am jealous.'

She laughed merrily. 'Don't forget I am the earl's housekeeper, Stephen.' She met his eyes. 'What has happened to put you in such a cheerful mood?'

'We've had a tantrum.'

Anthea stared. 'Whatever are you talking about?'

'Come out to the stables with me and I will tell you the story.'

'What will you say next? And what have the stables to do with the matter?' she asked him.

'Everything. I took Jennette out to see her new mare she is hoping to ride in the morning, by the way. Of course, Martha came too and never stopped burbling on . . .'

'Are you going to tell me what has happened?'

'All in good time, I think I will do a Miss Craddock on you—'

'Don't you dare,' she replied quickly.

'Jennette looked ravishing in a gown of pale blue with little embroidered knots on the skirt—I do notice these things.'

'Stephen.'

'Yes, I am getting to the point. Jennette

made a fuss of Tessa and I think perhaps she will be able to manage the mare who seemed quite docile with her—then we heard a little yelp coming from the out-building next to the stables and Jennette discovered the puppies.'

'The puppies?' Anthea was getting bewildered by this tale and thought that Stephen was deliberately trying to make an epic of it.

'Yes, Peg, the golden labrador, has had a litter and there are still two of the puppies left, the runt is an appealing little creature and Jennette fell in love with it.'

'Well, that's all right. I don't suppose the earl would object to Jennette having a dog with her when she goes walking or riding.'

Stephen's eyes were dancing. 'But Jennettte wanted to keep it in her bedroom.'

'Oh, no,' Anthea groaned and guessed what was coming.

'Oh, yes. Holly—she was named straight away—must go in the bedroom.'

'What did you say?'

'I didn't say anything, Martha said it all. No dogs in bedrooms for a young lady, and the wretched woman—and I know she is my cousin—went prosing on for half an hour as to how it wasn't suitable and not at all clean.'

Anthea still could not fully understand. 'But that wasn't unreasonable.'

'I know that, but our Jennette didn't agree. Stamped her foot, raised her voice—her aunt would have let her have a dog in her bedroom, she said.'

'Stephen, you didn't just stand by and let them have a scene?' said Anthea.

'Only for five minutes, then I stepped in. Played the heavy uncle and do you know that Jennette listened to me? Looked at me with those great blue eyes swimming with tears and and said "Very well, Stephen, I will do as you say. Holly can be my dog but she will stay out here in the stables".' He laughed and Anthea joined in his merriment. 'She's a minx, Anthea, a spoiled, wayward little minx. I do believe she only needs a firm hand, but she won't get it from Miss Craddock.'

'And you are a rogue, Stephen; you will be falling in love with her next.' Anthea was still laughing.

'And a lot of use that will do me when she is promised to Marcus.'

She nodded. 'Yes, he has been telling me. I must say I feel sorry for the girl, but she will be well looked after here, with both you and Marcus to keep her in order.'

'And Miss Craddock!'

'Oh dear, yes, Miss Craddock. I'd better have a word with her. She will be downcast if she thinks Jennette will pay no heed to her.'

He took her by the arm. 'Come out and see Jennette and the puppy first, they are quite a picture.'

Anthea thought Stephen was right when she saw Jennette sitting on the step of the out-building with the golden bundle of downy puppy on her lap. She looked up and smiled when she saw Anthea and Stephen.

'Oh, Mrs Davenport, do look, isn't she beautiful? And don't you think I might have been allowed to have her in my bedroom? Miss Craddock made such a fuss about it—'

'And you did not behave very well, Jennette.'

'Oh, Stephen has told you. But I do like my own way and no one was ever allowed to cross me at my aunt's because of poor Papa. Now Stephen has been very strict and I didn't dare to argue with him.'

Anthea had to bite her tongue not to laugh. 'Mr Lorimer was quite right, Jennette, and I hope you will see that the puppy will be better off out here with the other dogs.'

'Oh yes, I could see it when Stephen explained it to me. I am not stupid, you know, even though my aunt called me bird-witted, but I suppose I had better go and say I am sorry to Miss Craddock. I'm afraid she must be sulking and I must not be unkind to her.'

At this, Anthea felt there was no need for further reproof and her eyes met Stephen's across the pretty girl's head. Perhaps there is hope yet, they seemed to say to each other.

'I think the earl will be waiting for you in the drawing-room, Jennette. You go in and join him and I will fetch Miss Craddock.'

She watched as Jennette gently put the

91

puppy back with its mother and then got up to join Stephen, smiling up at him as they walked back into the house. She won't go far wrong if she has Stephen to keep an eye on her, Anthea said to herself, I do believe he is smitten with her, though I hope not. I like him too much to want to see him hurt by the girl he had described as a little minx.

Upstairs, Anthea found Miss Craddock sniffly and woebegone, but had the gratification of seeing the little spinster's expression change when she saw that it was the housekeeper who was wanting to speak with her.

'I am so glad to see you, Mrs Davenport, for I am quite shocked at Jennette's behaviour. I wonder if I am going to be able to handle her. It is becoming obvious that she is very wayward and wilful and that she was allowed too much of her own way in her aunt's house; her cousins were all boys except for the youngest little girl she shared a room with. I can only think that she has grown up with tomboyish ways. Fancy wanting to keep the dog in her bedroom, did you ever hear anything like it? And she would not listen to a word I said, just stamped her foot at me. I was never so shocked in all my life. It was a good job that Stephen was there—he always was one of my very favourite cousins, such a nice man—for he put his foot down and Jennette listened to him. So I left them to settle the puppy. I must say it is a dear little thing and reminds me of my poor Beth I had when I was a girl. But what am I going to do about Jennette if she is going to defy me? I really cannot tolerate such behaviour but I consider myself so lucky to be living at Felbeck Abbey and would hate to have to leave almost before I've arrived, if you see what I mean. What do you think, Mrs Davenport, I can see that you are a sensible woman?'

And past your last prayers, Anthea added wickedly. She had let Miss Craddock have her say thinking it would be better for the poor little dab of a woman to unload her anxieties.

'Miss Craddock, I think you can safely leave any discipline that Jennette might need to the earl and Mr Lorimer. You are here as her chaperon as it would not be proper for her to live in the house on her own with His Lordship. I would advise you to try not to argue with Jennette for I can see she is strong-willed and will only get the better of you. When she goes out, you will be with her, and in the house, you can sit quietly with your needlework or embroidery. Why don't you try some tapestry? The dining-room chairs are rather faded and could do with some new covers.'

Anthea had the satisfaction of seeing Miss Craddock's face brighten. 'Oh, what a good idea, Mrs Davenport, you are very practical. On our first shopping trip to York I will go to the linen-draper and buy some canvas and wools. I used to do tapestry years ago and I think I would enjoy it.'

They walked down to the drawing-room together and as Anthea opened the door, she was thankful to hear Jennette's words as Miss Craddock entered.

'Miss Craddock, we have settled Holly and I do apologize that I wouldn't listen to you . . .'

Then Anthea felt a hand on her arm and turned to find Stephen standing close to her. He had his fingers to his lips as though to tell her not to make a noise or to say anything. And so it was they both heard Jennette's apology to Miss Craddock and Anthea could see the relief in Stephen's face.

They shut the door and he spoke to her. 'In all the to-do about the puppy, Anthea, I forgot to ask you how you got on with Marcus, though I believe you described yourself as the housekeeper. Does that mean he is going to allow you to stay?' He smiled at her. 'I think you must be in favour or he would not have taken you to see the ruins of the old abbey; they are a kind of sacred place with him.'

Anthea could not tell Stephen even a tenth of what had happened between herself and the earl and she replied very briefly. 'He was not best pleased about Mrs Bailey but I think he could see the sense of it all. He is certainly very satisfied with what I have done in the house. So yes, Stephen, I am the new housekeeper of Felbeck Abbey.'

'And I think you could be its new mistress.'

Anthea thought he was funning. 'What a ridiculous thing to say. You know that Jennette is intended as the next Countess of Felbeck.'

He shook his head. 'I just cannot see it. I cannot see Jennette as Marcus's wife any more than I can see her as mistress of Felbeck Abbey.'

'She is young yet, Stephen; give her time to grow out of her childish tantrums and I think we might find a beautiful and polished young lady.'

He took her hand and raised it to his lips. 'You are as kind as you are clever.' Then he put his hand on the door-knob of the drawing-room. 'I think I had better join them for tea.'

If Anthea had thought that Jennette might have benefited from the contretemps over the puppy and her subsequent apology to Miss Craddock, she soon found herself sadly mistaken.

The very next morning, she was busy in the dairy when the sound of voices in argument came clearly to her. Looking out, she saw Jennette and the earl standing close to the dairy window. They were obviously on their way to the stables for both were dressed for riding. Jennette looked very fetching in a riding-habit of royal blue with gold frogging and braid around the cuffs. Rather spitefully for her, Anthea wondered if the young girl wore anything else but blue. As usual, the earl looked immaculate even though he was dresssed only for riding.

Anthea now found herself facing a dilemma. The pair were obviously in argument and she could hear every word from where she stood by the butter churn, but if she left the dairy by the only door, she would have to pass in front of them and she could feel the embarrassment of having to do so.

So she kept very still and listened. I'm eavesdropping, she said to herself, but perhaps it might be better if I can learn what the trouble is. Even after one day, she felt a sense of responsibility for Jennette's welfare and she was inclined to put it down to the ineptitude of Miss Craddock.

The trouble this morning seemed to be something to do with Jennette riding out on Tessa.

'No, I will not allow you to ride on your own, Jennette. If Miss Craddock is either unable or unwilling to ride then I will arrange for one of the stable boys to accompany you.' The earl sounded almost dictatorial, Anthea thought, and she could imagine the look on Jennette's face as the girl made her reply.

'I have already crossed with Miss Craddock on the matter, Marcus, she does not ride.'

'And she thinks you should not ride on your own?'

'So she said. I said I would ask you and now you are taking the same line. I have always ridden on my own if my cousins could not come with me. We were on the edge of Ashdown Forest, you know, and I was forever in the saddle. I thought it would be the same here.'

Anthea could sense that Marcus was making an effort to be both patient and reasonable. 'It is different now, Jennette. You are my ward and after your come-out, I hope to announce our betrothal. You are no longer a child with young cousins as your companions.'

'I don't think I want to marry you, Marcus; you are nearly old enough to be my father.'

Anthea held her breath and waited for the explosion of the earl's temper. But he surprised her with his patience with the child.

'That was not very graciously said, Jennette. I don't especially want to marry you but I promised your father. I think in a year's time when it becomes generally known that you are a considerable heiress, you will be glad of the protection of my name to keep the fortune-hunters at bay.'

'I might fall in love with someone else, Marcus.'

Little fool, thought Anthea. She is deliberately or ignorantly provoking him, I am not sure which it is. He'll never stand for such behaviour.

And the earl did not. 'Jennette,' he said, not angrily but very sternly and rather grimly, 'you are an orphan. You have had no formal upbringing and it is my intention to turn you into the beautiful young lady I think you could become and to take you as my wife. Love does not come into it, you will soon find that when you realize you have the chance of becoming the Countess of Felbeck. In the meantime, I have no objection to you going out riding on Tessa every day if you wish, but you go accompanied. Consider if you should take a toss, how would you fare if there was no one nearby to help you? You do not go alone, you understand?'

'Yes, Marcus, you are very strict, but I suppose I will get used to it.' There was a pause and then Jennette's voice became soft and winning. 'Do you not think that I am beautiful already?'

Anthea nearly burst out laughing. The silly chit, she thought.

'I think you pretty, yes, but you have none of the beauty that Mrs Davenport possesses for example.'

Anthea held her breath.

'Mrs Davenport? You think she is beautiful? Well, I know I am going to like her and she is very kind and quite handsome, in a way. But I would never call her beautiful: she is old.'

There was amusement in the earl's voice. 'It is quite obvious, my dear Jennette, that you do not hold older people in great esteem. That is a pity; I'm afraid you have a lot to learn. Do you think the same about my cousin,

Mr Lorimer?'

'Stephen? Oh no, he is so very handsome and he helped me to choose Tessa and came to my rescue when I had all that fuss with Miss Craddock about Holly. Oh Marcus, you haven't seen Holly yet, do come and have a look at her, she is a darling. I wonder if she will remember me.'

Anthea almost heard the earl's sigh. 'Very well, Jennette, and don't forget that I shall arrange for one of the stable boys to go with you when you ride. I think it will be Jed, he's a sensible lad and you will find him polite and helpful . . .'

Their voices faded as they moved off in the direction of the stables and Anthea quickly slipped back into the house. They say that eavesdroppers hear no good of themselves, she thought ruefully. All I have learned is that everything that Stephen said about Jennette is true. And also, for the third time, the earl has called me beautiful. He must be queer in the attic that's all I can think.

But lurking at the back of her mind was the memory of the kisses they had exchanged. I must learn to forget them as soon as possible, she told herself. I am the housekeeper and pleased with my duties and with the house; I shall consider it part of those duties to keep the Earl of Felbeck at a distance.

As the weeks went by and Anthea settled down to her new life, this last was to prove easier said than done.

In the first place, although he was glad enough to have Miss Craddock as a chaperon for his ward, the earl seemed to have no time or patience for Jennette himself. It became his practice to summon Anthea to his study after breakfast in the morning, to tell her his plans for the day and to make sure that Jennette was suitably occupied.

As Anthea had often done the same with her grandfather, she had no idea if it was a regular procedure with the aristocracy and found herself looking forward to that half-hour of friendly exchange of words. Often it would be her only social contact of the day and she valued it.

They did have occasional arguments and the first of these was about Jennette.

For Jennette, too, had settled down and seemed quite happy as long as she could ride out on Tessa, or take a walk, this last accompanied by Miss Craddock who proved to be a good walker and they went down the country lanes or over the fields with the growing, lolloping Holly at their heels. Jennette had been so far quite obedient about taking Jed with her on her rides and, in fact, the two had struck up an odd friendship; they were the same age and shared a love of the countryside.

Anthea came to the conclusion that the girl was an odd mixture: one minute the fashion-conscious young lady demanding to be taken to Mrs Peacock, the mantua-maker, in York to order a new gown; and the next coming home from her ride with shining excited eyes because they had seen some baby water voles at Hurns Beck. No, she had not let Holly go after them for they were sweet little things, she told Anthea happily.

The earl and Anthea were laughing at this incident one morning and wondering if Jennette would ever grow up. Jennette held her guardian somewhat in awe but could make herself charming if she wished to; with Stephen Lorimer it was a different matter.

The two were very close and Jennette seemed to turn to him in everything. Anthea had the feeling that Stephen kept an eye on Jennette as a big brother would; but on the other hand, it was not a brotherly look that she would sometimes see in his eyes if she caught him looking at Jennette unaware that he was being watched. I hope he is not going to get hurt, she would think, and knew she had said it to herself many times.

One particular morning, Anthea had no idea that she looked very striking and that when she entered the earl's study that he found that his breathing quickened.

As housekeeper, she wore very plain dresses with long sleeves which were full at the shoulders and tapered to the wrist. She wore no ornament but there was usually ruching or pleats on the bodice of the high-waisted dress which put it above the ordinary and showed her shapely and splendid figure to advantage.

One of her favourite dresses was of a rust colour that seemed to pick out the rich red light in her abundant hair; she wore no cap though she often thought that as housekeeper, she should have done.

Anthea,' said the earl, and she looked at him in surprise for he was always very formal and had only on that one occasion called her by name. 'No, don't protest. I hate having to call you Mrs Davenport. When we are alone, please allow me the privilege of saying your name.'

'It is not very businesslike, My Lord,' she replied. What else could she say?

'Be damned to business, these half-hours in the mornings set me up for the day. I love to look at you, I love to spar with you and I could wish that things were other than they are at the moment.'

She decided to ignore these remarks and concentrate on the arrangements for the day. 'Have you any plans for Jennette for today?' she asked.

'Yes, I will take her into York this afternoon. I think she wishes to purchase something at Bickers and Sowerby, the linen-drapers. And I must call and see my tailor.'

She looked at him rather surprised for his dress was so immaculate that she had always imagined that he used a London tailor. 'Not Stultz or Weston, My Lord?'

'You would have me the town beau, Mrs Davenport.'

'No, I think you dress very suitably for the country,' she replied and knew she was being familiar.

But the earl did not seem to object to her remark. 'You are gracious, Mrs Davenport. I patronize Mr Rhodes of Blake Street in York. He has a partner called Mr Malatrat who is an exceptional tailor, indeed he has an apprentice who was once with Weston. He is as good as any London tailor, but I am glad to have your approval.'

'As though the approval of the housekeeper mattered to you,' she rejoined.

Their eyes met. 'The approval of this particular housekeeper matters to me,' he said and his expression was intense.

Anthea was not thrown. Her feelings for this man were often turbulent but she managed to quell them under her guise as his housekeeper. 'Are you trying to flatter me into thinking that my opinions are important to you, My Lord,' she said lightly.

He did not reply but reached out and grasped her wrist with strong fingers. 'Everything about you is important to me,' he said and his tone was urgent.

Anthea felt the beating of her heart, but knew that they had got themselves on to dangerous ground and that she must some-how reverse the conversation. So she chose to misunderstand him.

'I do know how to order the servants; I can plan meals with the excellent Sarah and I must admit to keeping the house looking very nice.'

He grunted then and knew himself defeated. It was his ward he must put first and not his housekeeper.

'You are a paragon indeed, Mrs Davenport, and I am grateful for the gossiping letters of Mrs Tuke which brought you here in the first place.' He dropped his hand and sat back. Anthea gave a sigh of relief as the fraught and intimate moment receded. 'Now tell me your opinion about this come-out ball of Jennette's. I know very little about such things.'

Anthea had already given it some consideration and had no hesitation in telling the earl what her thoughts on the subject were. 'We are coming up to Christmas and the months after the festivities are usually rather cold and dreary ones. I think the best thing to do is to hold the ball right at the start of the next season in the spring. Maybe at about the same time as the spring race meeting when everyone will be in town. You have a town house, My Lord?' It was something Anthea had never enquired about.

'Yes, there is a Lorimer house in Petergate but we have never used it as we are only four miles from the city. It has been let out to the same family for years. Do you think we have need of it?'

Anthea considered. 'It would have been useful for Jennette to reach Mrs Peacock, her mantua-maker, more easily, but as we have successfully done that by taking the carriage in from Felbeck Abbey, I don't think it signifies. In any case, Jennette would not want to be parted from her beloved Tessa and Holly!'

'She does enjoy that ride, doesn't she?' he smiled. 'I wonder if I should take her round the farms with me, or even let Stephen do it.'

'I think there is plenty of time for that,' she replied.

'You mean after our marriage?'

Anthea looked up sharply. There had been an odd note in his voice and it made her wonder if the idea of being wedded to the young Jennette was irksome to him. 'I believe you are thinking that Jennette is rather young to be taking up the duties of being countess, but she will be nineteen years of age on her next birthday and I think I can see an improvement in her childish ways already.' She knew she was being outspoken but there was a candid directness between her and the earl which allowed her to say such things.

'I am glad you think so, Mrs Davenport,' he said rather sardonically. 'I must confess I have failed to notice it. She is not like you.'

Anthea instantly blazed with indignation. 'Of course she is not like me, what a preposterous thing to say. I am nearly ten years her senior and I am in a position of some responsibility . . .' She stopped, appalled. 'I am sorry, My Lord, I am being presumptuous.'

He rose from his chair, put out a hand, grasped hers and pulled her to her feet and Anthea found herself standing close to him and looking into amused eyes. 'It is what I like about you, for you are not afraid to say what you think. So I am preposterous, am I? Shall I demand a forfeit for that remark?'

'Whatever are you talking about?' she returned.

'It is not usual for a housekeeper to call her employer preposterous, Mrs Davenport.'

'I apologize, My Lord.' But Anthea did not feel apologetic, neither did she feel subservient and knew herself to be at fault.

'You will allow me my forfeit then?' he teased, his face close to hers. She knew instantly what he meant.

She tried to move away but it was too late. His hands were round her waist and she was drawn up against him. To struggle away would have been undignified and in any case, her body was telling her that it wanted to be close to the earl. Then she stopped thinking as his lips found hers, deeply searching until at last she gave way and surrendered herself to him.

When they drew apart, they hardly dared to look at one another for that same passion had been aroused between them before and it was a passion they could not admit to feeling.

Anthea forced herself to be calm in spite of the torment of her feelings. 'I think I have paid my forfeit in full, My Lord. I will go about my duties.'

And without looking at him again, she let herself out of the room then stood outside leaning against the door to get her breath and her composure back.

She was not to know that back inside the study, the earl had sat himself at his desk, his head buried in his hands.

She is bewitching, he was saying to himself, she is the one who should be my wife, not that silly chit of a girl who is my ward.

CHAPTER SIX

Winter was closing in but there was no snow and Jennette continued her morning rides. If she felt she should be more in society, she did not say so for she knew that the time of her come-out ball would be soon after Christmas.

Then in the space of an hour, on a morning of pale wintry sunshine and dry ground, early in December, she met Merrick Downes and promptly fell in love.

She was riding across Hall Moor which stretched invitingly as far as the village of Shipton and was one of her favourite places for a gallop, when she felt Tessa go lame. She slowed and jumped off the horse without being aided, looking around for Jed who was never far away. But instead of the figure of the small Jed on his black mare, another rider approached her and she could see instantly from the splendid hunter which he was riding, and from the cut of his riding-coat that he was a gentleman of some degree of fashion.

As he drew closer, she saw with excitement that he was indeed a gentleman and not only young, but very handsome. His head was bare and his black hair blew carelessly in the wind. He smiled as he dismounted and looked concerned.

'Are you in trouble, ma'am, is there any way I can help you?'

Jennette knew that it was wrong to talk to a gentleman to whom she had not been introduced and hesitated when she made her reply. 'Thank you,' she said rather stiffly. 'I have my stable-boy, Jed, with me. He will soon be here.'

The newcomer laughed. 'You have been told that it is not proper to talk to strange gentlemen! May I introduce myself?'

Their eyes met, Jennette's very blue and sparkling at the encounter, the young man's dark and admiring. At that moment, Jed came galloping up and quickly took in the scene.

As he jumped down, he looked first at his mistress. 'Is everything all right, Miss

Jennette? I thought Tessa was going lame.'

'Yes, she is; this gentleman stopped to offer his help.'

Jed looked from one to the other not sure what was the correct thing to do. I suppose I'd better introduce them, he said to himself.

'Miss Jennette, this is Mr Merrick Downes of Downes Hall near Skelton. You know it, for it is that big stone house we pass sometimes if we are riding that way.' Then he turned to the young man. 'Mr Merrick, this is Miss Jennette Goodison, she is the earl's ward, you know.' That was all Jed had to say but he thought he had done quite well.

Merrick Downes stood in front of Jennette and made his bow as though he had been in the drawing-room. 'Miss Goodison, I had heard that the earl had his ward staying with him. Had I known she was so beautiful, I would have not lingered in London.'

Jennette liked this and gave a radiant smile. 'You like to flatter, sir, I am sure my looks are no more than pretty.' Then she thought she had been too forward, but this was fun. 'I think I have heard my guardian speak of your family, sir, and that he knows Mr Downes well. I was not aware that there was a son of your age.'

Merrick laughed. 'All my brothers and sisters are married and left home. I'd better warn you that I am the wastrel of the family.'

Jennette was delighted. 'I've never met a wastrel before, you don't look like one to me

109

for you are very fashionable.'

'Miss Goodison, I think we were destined to meet. Are you an heiress, by any chance? I am desperate to meet with a beautiful heiress for my pockets are to let and I have had to come home for funds.'

'I will be an heiress next year, but I am afraid my fortune is closely guarded by the earl.'

'You mean Marcus, Earl of Felbeck? He is your guardian?'

She nodded. 'Yes, he is going to present me next year and then we will be betrothed.'

Her remark was met with laughter. 'So he is keeping your fortune to add to his own overflowing coffers. Wise man. I hope he is generous.'

'Oh yes,' she replied. 'He meets all my bills for the modiste and mantua-maker but I have very little pin-money.'

'Never mind. Now I think I will accompany you back to Felbeck Abbey. I have known Marcus all my life, you know, but I have been fixed in London for a year so I did not know he was back from the Continent. However, I heard that the old earl had died. Now what are we going to do about your horse? What is her name, did you say?'

'It is Tessa. She suddenly went lame so she may have cast a shoe.'

Jed suddenly interrupted. 'Miss Jennette, if you don't me suggesting, I could lead Tessa

110

home if Mr Merrick would kindly take you up in front of him. It is too far for you to walk.'

Jennette looked doubtfully at the young Mr Downes and found that he was nodding his approval. 'Yes, that is a good idea. Do you think you could manage on Dexter if I held on to you?'

'I think I could; will you help me to mount?'

There is nothing more likely to create an instant liking and friendship than a pretty girl riding on a horse and being held round the waist by a handsome young man. They went along slowly and by the time they had reached Felbeck Abbey, they had decided that they could dispense with the 'sir' and 'ma'am' and they were Merrick and Jennette to one another.

Jed had ridden on, leading Tessa to tell them at the house what had happened, so Anthea was on the look-out for them. She had told the earl of the mishap.

She had seen the frown come into his eyes for a brief second then he seemed to dismiss it. 'Merrick Downes? Is he home? He must be in Dun Territory and has come home for a while. There is no harm in him; I've known him since he was in leading-strings. He's grown up rather a loose screw with a taste for gaming. Very much the dandy and very handsome, Jennette is sure to fall in love with him.'

But when Merrick handed Jennette down from his horse, Marcus was there to meet

111

them. 'Good of you, Merrick,' he said pleasantly. 'You home on a repairing lease?'

Merrick laughed. 'Something like that, Marcus. I must say that it is very nice to be here again and to meet with Miss Goodison. Understand she is your ward. Have to congratulate you?'

'Not quite yet,' Marcus replied. 'I think Jennette must get used to the ways of a big house like Felbeck Abbey first. Come along in and we'll get some ale brought for us.' He turned to Jennette. 'I am sorry about Tessa, but they will see to her in the stables and she'll be as right as rain by tomorrow morning.'

'I didn't mind, Marcus, for it means I have met Merrick.'

'Merrick already, is it?' her guardian quizzed her. 'But I suppose you young people do not like too much formality.'

They all moved into the house, where they found Miss Craddock fussing round like an old hen.

'Are you sure you have come to no harm, Jennette dear? I knew I was right to insist that you had someone to ride with you and fortunately Marcus agreed with me. But I must admit to some alarm when I saw Jed leading your horse back. And this is Mr Merrick Downes? I have met your mother, Mr Downes, a very pleasant lady. She will be pleased to have you at home, I am sure. And now here is Mrs Davenport come to see what all the fuss is about, she is our housekeeper, you know, and runs the place like clockwork. I'm sure I don't know what we would do without her . . . Mrs Davenport, this is Mr Merrick Downes who kindly went to Jennette's rescue. He is from Downes Hall, you know, that big stone house on the way to Skelton . . .'

Anthea thought it best to put a stop to Miss Craddock's flow. She had already seen the glances that were passing between Jennette and Merrick and sensed trouble ahead.

'Mr Downes, I am pleased to meet you. The earl has asked me to say that there is a nuncheon prepared if you would care to stay.'

Merrick looked at Jennette but hesitated before replying. 'I thank you, but I think I must be on my way or my mother will be thinking I have met with an accident.'

Anthea thought it properly said and began to think more highly of the young man she had at first thought little more than a dandy.

'I will send one of the servants with a message for Mrs Downes,' she said. 'Please come into the breakfast-room, it will be less formal than the dining-room as you are still in your riding clothes.'

Jennette gave a little frown. 'Do you think I should go and change into a morning dress, Miss Craddock?' she asked her chaperon.

It was Merrick who replied. 'You look lovely in that blue riding-habit, Jennette, there is no need to change for me. I hope to continue our acquaintance and to see you in one of your pretty dresses many times to come.'

Anthea thought the remark over-familiar for such a short acquaintance but Jennette glowed. 'Oh, Merrick,' she said, smiling into his eyes. 'I do hope so.'

It was to be the beginning of a friendship that lasted the whole winter. Jennette was allowed to ride with Merrick on her own as Marcus seemed to regard the young man more as a brotherly companion than as a handsome tearaway who had managed to capture Jennette's affection in no more than a few days.

Anthea could see that Jennette was in thrall to the young man and it was the cause of her first serious disagreement with her employer. Miss Craddock, for some reason known only to herself, approved of Jennette's friendship with Merrick. She often left them on their own in the drawing-room when it would have been more proper for her to have played her real role as chaperon.

They had a spell of snowy weather in the middle of January and the daily rides were impossible; Merrick arrived in the Downes carriage. He always dressed to a fault and Jennette was seen to admire his brightly coloured breeches and flashy waistcoats, his high shirt points and his elaborate neck-cloths.

On a day when Jennette and Merrick had been left on their own in the drawing-room,

Anthea went into the room to make sure that the fire in the big Tudor firelace was properly attended to.

She noticed immediately that the pair were sitting close together on the high-backed settle which was drawn up to the fire and that they jumped apart as she entered. The cushions which made the settle a more comfortable place to sit had fallen to the floor together with Jennette's Kashmir shawl. Jennette was flushed and her hair tumbled and Merrick rather than looking guilty at what was obviously ungentlemanly behaviour, greeted Anthea with some attempt at levity.

'Don't you think that Jennette is looking prettier than ever, Mrs Davenport? I have been telling her that the cold weather has brought roses to her cheeks.'

As Jennette was breathing rather quickly as though recovering from a passionate embrace, Anthea spoke rather coolly. 'It is a pity that the weather is not fit for you to ride, you would be better occupied in the saddle.'

Jennette, obviously guilty, took Anthea to task for her censure. 'It is for my guardian to say whether Merrick is welcome here when the weather is bad. You are only the housekeeper and have nothing to say in the matter.'

Anthea stiffened for she knew Jennette was right but Merrick, sensing an awkward situation, was at his most charming.

'Mrs Davenport, I have been trying to

persuade Jennette to let me show her how to play chess but she refuses. Don't you think it would be a good pastime for these wintry days?'

As Anthea had to agree, she tried to reply civilly. 'It is a good idea, Merrick; there is a chess table in the library and I will have it moved into the drawing-room if you would like that. Why don't you give it a try, Jennette?'

The girl was still pouting, obviously put out at being found in a compromising situation with her hero of the moment. 'I will ask Stephen what he thinks,' was all she said.

Anthea left them with the last remark ringing in her ears for it was an odd fact that since Jennette's friendship with Merrick had begun, she had turned more and more to Stephen rather to her guardian. I think she is rather afraid of the earl, thought Anthea; she is in need of a confidante and obviously does not count Miss Craddock as a friend in that sense, for she knew that the chaperon would simply read her charge a lecture when she was in need of advice; but Stephen is a different matter. He is very fond of the girl, I can tell, and she has always listened to him right from the time he helped her to choose Tessa.

Anthea found Stephen in his office seemingly busy with the farm accounts. She had discovered him to be an efficient steward with a genuine love of the acres and farms of Felbeck Abbey.

He looked up and smiled as she knocked and entered.

'Hello, my Anthea, what can I do for you? Are you looking worried by any chance?'

'Why do you always call me "my Anthea"?' she asked him.

He laughed. 'I think it is because it was me that found you and brought you from Carlisle. That was a good day for us all.'

'You flatter, Stephen.'

'No, it is the truth, for I know that Marcus holds you in very high esteem. But it is not Marcus who has brought the frown to your eyes, is it our little minx?'

'Yes, it is. I never quite approved of the freedom given to Merrick when he visits Jennette, but it is nothing to do with me. I have noticed that she turns to you a lot, Stephen, and I believe that you are more than a little fond of her.'

'Yes, I am, for my sins. What has she been up to now?'

'I've just found her in Merrick's arms in the drawing-room and it was obvious from her face and her clothing that it was not just a polite kiss. I rather took her to task, though it was not my place, and when Merrick suggested—rather sensibly to my surprise— that they should play chess together, Jennette's reply was that she would ask you.'

Stephen had moved from his desk to the fireplace. 'Come and sit with me, Anthea, and we will talk it over. I think you are right to be concerned.'

Anthea sat down and looked across at him struck, not for the first time, by his straight handsome features and neat fair hair so much like Jennette's. 'What does she tell you, Stephen? She comes to you rather than to anyone else.'

He laughed. 'She treats me as though I am her favourite uncle! I don't mind that for I think it is good for her to have someone she can trust and turn to.'

'Why does she not go to the earl?'

'Marcus puzzles me. He is very good to her; I think in his own way, he is quite fond of her, but he thinks of her still as a child. Yet in a few months' time, he is talking about being betrothed to her. A promise made like the one to her father is very important and serious to him.'

Anthea was thoughtful. 'Yet she would not run to him if she was in trouble?'

'No, I am sure she would not, she would come to me. You know she thinks she is wildly in love with Merrick, don't you?' he asked her.

'I guessed as much. Her whole life is bound up with when Merrick will come and what Merrick will say.' She paused and knew she must say the next words. 'I don't trust him, Stephen.'

'Why do you say that, my Anthea?'

'I'm not sure what it is. He is very much the

118

dandy which I suppose is something I dislike and he admitted to having come home because of his gambling debts. I suppose he expected his father to settle them for him. He is the youngest son and has been spoiled in very much the same way as Jennette was spoiled by her aunt.'

'In fact, they are a pair!'

She managed a laugh. 'Yes, I suppose so. They are never far apart and I must say that Jennette is very happy in his company. I half expected her to be difficult cooped up here for the winter and not yet in society, but it has been the other way round. I suppose I am silly to worry about the girl and it really is no concern of mine. I just hope that Merrick doesn't lead her astray.'

'I will keep an eye on her. You will have to admit that it is good that she does come to me even if she thinks I am an elderly uncle.'

Anthea did laugh then. 'Anyone less like an uncle than you would be hard to imagine, Stephen.'

She went away reassured by Stephen's words and opinions, and with a promise from him that he, himself, would move the chess table into the drawing-room. Also that he would give Jennette a few lessons so that she would be able to enjoy a game with Merrick.

It was not to be the last conversation on the topic of Jennette's behaviour that day, but Anthea was to find that her interview with the earl was not as successful as the one with Stephen.

She was in her sitting-room early that afternoon thinking about dinner menus to discuss with Sarah when there was a knock on the door and a smiling Earl of Felbeck stepped into the room.

'You should be out of doors on a lovely day like this,' he said without even greeting her.

'But it has been snowing,' she replied.

'And haven't you noticed that the snow has ceased and the sun is shining and everywhere outside is beautiful? Have you got thick boots?'

He is in a strange mood, she thought, before she replied. 'Yes, I have some sturdy half-boots; I always walked in the snow in Cumberland.'

'Well, go and put them on, find a warm pelisse and bonnet and come for a walk with me.'

'My Lord . . .' she started, but was quickly interrupted.

'No arguments. An earl cannot walk with his housekeeper, you were going to say and I shall disregard it. On the other hand, an earl can give orders to his housekeeper, come to think of it. Mrs Davenport, put on your boots and come for a walk with me.'

She had to smile at his words but she had one more objection to make. 'But would you rather not take Jennette?'

'I would not. She is closeted in the drawing-room with Merrick, in any case. They seem to be arguing as to whether he should teach her to play chess or not, so I left them to it.'

She gave in at last. Perhaps it will give me an opportunity to say something on the subject of Jennette and Merrick, she told herself.

She ran upstairs and it took no more than a few minutes to get into her half-boots and to slip into a heavy dark-brown pelisse which she kept for this kind of weather. Velvet bonnet and kid gloves and she was ready and running down the stairs to find the earl waiting by the front door.

'Good girl,' was all he said.

As soon as she was outside, Anthea felt glad. The sky was a pale blue but the sun was shining and the gardens and grounds looked beautiful. The snow had not been heavy but there had been enough to settle on trees and shrubs forming lovely shapes and patterns wherever she looked.

'Yes, it's beautiful, isn't it?'

Anthea had almost forgotten her companion but she looked up at him and smiled. 'I have always loved to see the sun on the fresh snow, it's like magic.'

'You are like magic.'

She looked at him astonished. 'Whatever are you saying?'

'Your brown eyes are glowing like magic and I want to kiss your lovely mouth.'

Anthea stopped short, thinking that the earl must have taken leave of his senses. 'I think I had better forgo the walk if you are going to talk in that vein. I've had enough trouble for one day.'

'No, I will behave, I promise you. We will take a walk to the abbey ruins though we cannot sit on the stones today.' He stepped out briskly at her side, a commanding figure in top boots, an overcoat of drab with several capes and a tall black hat. 'Now what is all this about trouble today? Is it something to do with the servants? I trust the cook has not left us. I know I always leave these things in your safe hands, but it does not mean that they do not interest me. Anything that affects you, affects me also.'

Anthea was finding it quite difficult to keep up with him and quite unable to fathom either his mood or his words. She wondered if it would be wise to mention his ward to him.

'Well, are you going to tell me about all this trouble?'

'My Lord, if I am going to tell you anything at all then you had better slow down. I do like walking in the crisp snow but I cannot keep up with your pace.'

She saw him glance down at her and thought his smile was somewhat tender and enigmatic.

'I was thinking about something else. I am sorry.'

'There is no need to apologize, it was natural for you to want to walk quickly and generally I could keep up with you. I am considered a good walker.' She stopped and looked about her. They were nearing the abbey ruins which looked picturesque with their stones capped with snow. 'It seems a pity to spoil that lovely expanse of snow with our footprints, doesn't it?'

He, too, stopped. 'Would you like us to walk round the edge to leave the snow in its pristine glory?'

'No, of course not, it was only an idle thought.' This is a ridiculous conversation, she was saying to herself, I came out to talk to him about Jennette.

She followed him to the corner of the ruins which was sheltered and was catching the rare warmth of that January sunshine.

'Now you can tell me what is troubling you.' It was like an order which must be obeyed.

'It is Jennette.'

'It is Jennette?' he echoed, and she thought his tone held some exasperation. 'And what has Jennette to do with you, Mrs Davenport? She is *my* ward.'

'Jennette's affairs have nothing to do with me,' she replied hastily. 'As you say, she is your ward and she has Miss Craddock as her chaperon and companion. She also has the confidence of Mr Lorimer.'

'So I have noticed, but I fail to see what it

123

has to do with you.'

'It would have nothing to do with me if I had not come across Mr Downes making love to her in the drawing-room this morning; her clothing was disarrayed and she looked flushed and excited.'

There was a silence, then he seemed to shrug his shoulders. 'What if Merrick should steal a kiss, there is no harm in the lad except a young man's propensity for gambling. Even he had the sense to come home when he wasn't flush in the pockets. I have been glad to see him as a riding companion for Jennette this winter, I think it has been most suitable.'

'You think it suitable for your intended bride to ride out with another man?' Even as she said it, Anthea knew she had over-stepped the mark.

'You dare to criticize my opinion, Mrs Davenport?' His tone was frigid.

'I apologize. It was not intended as a criticism. It worries me that Jennette will commit some indiscretion in her young ignorance.'

'I think you may leave Jennette's affairs to me, ma'am. I am of the opinion that she will come to no harm with Merrick; the Downes are much respected in the neighbourhood and any friendship with their son can only reflect well on Jennette.' Both his tone and his manner were stiff and Anthea hardly knew what to do or say to get them out of this impasse.

She decided that only forthrightness on her part would serve. 'Jennette says she is in love with Merrick,' she told him in what she thought was a common-sense kind of way.

He laughed at her. 'Jennette will be in and out of love a dozen times before she becomes my wife, it will do her no harm. Perhaps it will only serve to remove some of the silliness from her demeanour.'

'You find her silly, My Lord? Most men are taken with her beauty.' Anthea hardly knew why she was arguing with the earl except that his attitude over Jennette seemed very lax and it was not like him.

She was not to know that the earl could not care less about Jennette's behaviour with Merrick, thinking of it as only an innocent pastime between two young people. It was not Jennette that concerned him most, it was his housekeeper.

And before Anthea knew what was happening, he had put gloved fingers to her throat, deftly undone the ribbons of her bonnet and taken it off. He held it carefully with one hand and with the other he lifted her chin so that he could look into her eyes. She faced him proudly.

'Mrs Davenport,' he said slowly and carefully, 'we have talked about beauty before and you are aware that yours is the only kind of beauty I admire.' She dared not move, afraid of betraying the swift rush of emotion which had swept through at his touch. 'I think, ma'am, if Merrick can steal a kiss from my ward that I might be allowed one from my housekeeper. Give me your lips.'

Slowly and deliberately, his lips moved on hers. Her little stir of movement away from him served only to excite him for he dropped her bonnet in the snow and pulled her close to him. His hands slid skilfully beneath her pelisse and she felt the urgency of his fingers on the fine wool of her dress beneath. His lips became urgent, too, and Anthea once again gave herself to the passion she had experienced before and had so often forced herself to forget.

When he let her go, he whispered her name. 'Anthea, would that it were otherwise.'

She chose to ignore his remark which she scarcely understood. She felt weak and had a longing to lean against him and feel his strong body support her. But it was she herself who must have the strength and must somehow find a way to pass off the intimate moment. I must make sure I am never on my own with him again, she was saying to herself, he is too attractive to me and I can feel myself coming to love him.

So she simply stated the obvious. 'The sun has almost gone, My Lord.'

He bent to pick up her bonnet, brushed off the snow and tied the ribbons under her chin.

Then pulling her hand through his arm, he walked with her through the ruins. 'It is a good job that one of us has their feet firmly on the ground. You tempt me beyond endurance. I must be careful not to be on my own with you for I cannot answer for my behaviour.'

And he did not know that he had almost echoed Anthea's own thoughts and feelings.

CHAPTER SEVEN

The snow lay for a week and in that time, Jennette did learn to play chess; she and Merrick also went for long walks together and were as close and affectionate as ever. Stephen was keeping an eye on them and Jennette still confided in him; indeed he was the first one to hear about it when Merrick made Jennette an offer of marriage.

The dark days slipped by and they were soon into April and making plans for Jennette's come-out ball which would take place at the Assembly Rooms in York during the first week in May.

Jennette and Merrick were talking about the ball one morning on one of their riding trips. They had gone towards Hall Moor and as the ground rose and they were afforded a view of the River Ouse winding to the great hall at Beningbrough, they sat under the trees and sent the horses off to graze.

'Only a month to go, Jennette,' said Merrick suddenly. He was sitting with his back against a tree and had his arm around her. She had discarded her riding hat and was leaning her fair head against his chest. Idly, he stroked her curls and Jennette liked the feel of his fingers in her hair.

'You mean my ball?' she asked him.

'Yes, what else? It is the great event of the season!'

She gave a giggle. 'It is for us, I suppose. But my ball gown is not ready yet; wait till you see it, Merrick.'

'Will I love you more than ever?' he said, half teasing.

'Do you love me now?' she asked him.

His arm tightened round her. 'You know I do for I have told you so many times. I only wish it could be for ever.'

She turned in his arms, knelt beside him and tried to see if he was being serious. 'What do you mean?'

He replied carefully. 'I know we are both young but I would like to marry you, Jennette.'

'Merrick.'

He put his hands round her face and kissed her lips very slowly and sweetly. 'Would you marry me, Jennette, I know you love me?'

She gave a deep sigh. 'There is nothing I would like better, but I have been properly brought up and I know that you should ask my guardian's permission to address me, Merrick.'

He protested, 'But that is just what I cannot do. You know very well he talks of you becoming betrothed to him after your come-out. He would never countenance an offer from me.'

'But he might if he knew we really loved each other as much as we do. He only wishes for my happiness, I am sure.'

But Merrick looked gloomy. 'He made that promise to your papa, you told me so. Marcus is a man of honour and would never renege on a promise such as that.'

'I think he would give his permission if he knew I was in earnest and we asked him properly.' She looked at the young man to whom she had lost her heart so quickly. 'In any case, Merrick, you are not in a position to marry. As a younger son you have no expectations, have you?'

He shook his head. 'No, none at all, but it does not signify for there is your fortune. Do you come into your inheritance on your birthday?'

Jennette felt a sudden chill of doubt; she had been so certain and sure in her love. 'Merrick, do you mean you are wanting to marry me for my inheritance? I have to wait until my twenty-first birthday, you know.'

He looked startled but made a hurried recovery; he kissed her quickly and said even more quickly, 'No, I do love you, but we

129

cannot live without some financial means and I have nothing. If we could get Marcus's consent, perhaps he would release your money to you before you are one-and-twenty. He would not wish to see you living without funds.'

'No, you are quite right,' she replied. 'He is very generous even though I haven't got to know him very well. I find that Stephen is much more easy-natured.'

He smiled. 'I think Stephen admires you; don't go falling in love with him, Jennette.'

'As if I would when I have you,' she protested indignantly. 'Ask Marcus when you have the opportunity. It would make me so happy, Merrick, to think we could be betrothed. Perhaps we could announce it at my come-out.'

'You are a darling girl,' he said, as he pulled her back into his arms. 'Let me show you how much I love you.'

'No, no, Merrick . . . you are too rough . . . oh, Merrick . . .' Jennette wound her arms round his neck and let him kiss her in a way which would have shocked Miss Craddock and Anthea, too, had she known of it.

Even the forward Jennette seemed to be aware that her behaviour was not proper for a young girl and she pulled herself from his arms when she felt his fingers stray from her face to her body.

'Oh no, Merrick, we must not. I am sure it is

wrong of us to be sitting here on our own when we are thought to be enjoying a ride. I am afraid Miss Craddock would be very shocked.'

He sat up straight and gave a laugh. 'It would take very little to shock Miss Craddock, I fear.' Then he stood up and helped her to her feet. 'Come along, you little hussy, I must teach myself to wait for you.'

When they had ridden home and Merrick had left to go back to Downes Hall, Jennette went in search of Stephen. He was just back from his visit to the farms and looked wind-blown and handsome in his riding clothes.

'I want to talk to you, Stephen.'

'Come into the office, Jennette; you look worried about something.'

Stephen Lorimer was more than fond of Jennette. He had loved her on first seeing her, then despaired of her young and foolish ways, finally wanting nothing more than to take her in his arms and guard her and love her for the rest of his life.

He had never been anything but circumspect with her for he knew that she both trusted him and turned to him in every little matter. He had told Anthea that he felt as though Jennette thought of him as an uncle but he did not mind even this. If he could save her from her own foolishness, he would be satisfied.

'Well, what is it?' he asked, thinking she was going to tell him that one of her new dresses had been delivered to her with a pink bow instead of a blue one; such were the little problems she liked to share with him.

Jennette had meant to talk sensibly to Stephen but her words were suddenly blurted out. 'Merrick wants to marry me.'

Stephen stared, thinking he had heard wrongly. He went round the desk, sat by her side and took her hand in his.

'Tell me.'

It all poured out then, and Stephen found himself having to put all the words in order to make sense of what she was telling him.

'He says he loves me and I love him. And we would have my inheritance because he has no income of his own. We would announce it at my come-out. And he is going to ask Marcus, but I told him I was already promised to Marcus. He says he thinks Marcus will change his mind about wanting to marry me when he knows how much I love Merrick. He's very handsome and dresses to a fault, doesn't he? And I do love him, Stephen, and I don't think he wants to marry me for my fortune. He kissed me, you see.'

Stephen did see. And he felt dismayed. He knew Merrick Downes for an engaging, likeable rascal who had bewitched Jennette the whole winter. Now the game he was playing had become obvious. His gallantry had been nothing more than a ruse to get at Jennette's fortune. Slow down, Stephen, he said to himself, don't let her see how concerned you are. Merrick Downes has Marcus to contend with; I don't think that Marcus would ever let Jennette marry in such a way. She is still only eighteen and often seems younger.

So Stephen did his best not to alarm Jennette. Any opposition would make the wayward girl do the exact opposite to what one wished for her. 'Jennette,' he said gently, putting both his hands round hers. 'You don't need to rush into marriage with Merrick. Let him ask for Marcus's permission to address you then, if you still love him when your season is over, and Marcus will release you, you and Merrick can announce your betrothal. You never know, you might meet a marquis at one of the balls and fall in love with him!'

Jennette gave a sigh. 'I can't imagine being married to a marquis, but it would be very grand, wouldn't it?' She gripped his hands. 'Oh, Stephen, you always think of the right things and you are right again this time. Of course there is no need to rush into a marriage with Merrick, I'm not going to stop loving him. But I am looking forward to my season in York, it will be fun and Merrick can enjoy it, too. I will leave it all to Marcus. He will know what to say to Merrick when the time comes. Thank you, Stephen, you are a true friend. Can I give you a kiss?'

'I think you've probably had enough kisses

for one day,' he replied drily.

She smiled. 'That was different,' she said and reached up and her soft lips touched his cheek and Stephen had to be content.

The great occasion of Jennette's ball was soon upon them, but a week before the event found the earl and his housekeeper in conflict.

Their morning meetings and settling of the day's matters had continued and on each occasion, Anthea found a little more to like in Marcus Lorimer. Some of the more dangerously emotional experiences of the past did not arise again and she appreciated his friendship and his amiable teasing.

That was until the day he told her he expected her to be a guest at Jennette's come-out ball. His first question on the matter slipped easily from him and had Anthea completely puzzled.

'Well, Mrs Davenport, that's today settled,' he said, as she was about to leave the study. 'Have you chosen which gown to wear?'

Anthea was standing at the study door, her hand on its knob; the earl had stepped to stand in front of his desk, and business matters finished with, he was smiling at her.

'I fail to understand you, My Lord,' she replied and looked at his face to see if she could find a clue to the odd statement.

'Your gown for Jennette's ball,' he said.

'But I am not going to Jennette's ball.' Her tone was impatient.

'Of course you are going, what are you thinking of?'

'I am thinking that you've got windmills in your head. A house-keeper does not attend the come-out ball of the daughter of the house.'

He stepped forward, put out a hand and grasped her round the wrist.

'This housekeeper is going to.' There was a note of steel in his voice.

'This housekeeper is not.' She said it hotly, feeling her temper rising swiftly and that was unusual for her.

He changed tactics, pulled her gently towards him and became almost cajoling, not like the earl she had come to know. 'Anthea, you have been my housekeeper for six months and your services are much appreciated. I have told you so many times. Jennette looks to you rather than to Miss Craddock and she would be upset if you did not join in the celebration.'

Their eyes met and Anthea did not let her gaze drop. She knew very well what was right and wrong when it came to the etiquette of such things, and nothing would move her.

But she had to convince the Earl of Felbeck. 'My Lord, I am not saying that I would not like to attend the ball, nothing would give me greater pleasure, but I am your housekeeper. Do I have to repeat it? It is not my place to be there and it would shock your friends and acquaintances if I were. It is quite beyond my understanding that you should even think of such a thing and I wish to hear no more about it. The subject is closed.'

'I want to kiss you.'

The words dropped boldly into the argument and Anthea knew an instant flare of passion.

'You are insulting, My Lord. I may be your housekeeper, but I am no ordinary servant.' Anthea said the words through gritted teeth; she could feel her heart thumping and her wrist was still held fast in his hand.

'You are no ordinary housekeeper, my goose, you are Miss Anthea Davenport of Loxley Hall and you know it. I would like you to be by my side in the Assembly Rooms, but I suppose it will have to be that little squab of a cousin of mine.'

Anthea took Miss Craddock's part, glad of a shift in the subject and a lessening of the tension between them. 'Miss Craddock is a Lorimer. She is also fond of Jennette in her own way, even if she has little control over the girl. She would be shocked at your suggesting that I should attend the ball; she will be proud to be there herself, she speaks of little else.'

He dropped her hand and she was relieved that the awkward moment was over. 'You consider that I let Jennette run too wild?' he asked suddenly. 'I did not want to appear the overstrict guardian, she is very young.'

'Jennette has come to no harm so far and I

expect that after her come-out, her circle of friends will widen and that she will be invited to routs and parties and be generally accepted in York society. There is no denying her beauty.' Anthea regretted the words as soon as she had said them for she knew very well that her remark would provoke him.

And she was right.

'I think you had better leave, Mrs Davenport, before I ravish you.'

She caught a glimmer of laughter in his voice but when she spoke, her tone was stiff. 'If you have no more instructions for me, I will go about my duties.' And she left the room without looking at him again.

For the next few days, Anthea found herself caught up in the whirl of preparations for the ball and almost wished she had let the earl persuade her into going.

Then two days before the event, there arose a minor crisis which caused yet another argument between Marcus and his house-keeper.

Miss Craddock, who had looked forward to the occasion so much, was taken ill with a putrid sore throat and when Anthea summoned the Lorimers' doctor from York, he declared that Miss Craddock was not to leave her bed. He left strict instructions not to let her go into society or anywhere near Jennette for fear of spreading the infection.

The little woman had a high fever and when

Anthea took her some fresh barley water, she found the patient worried and rambling.

'Thank you, Mrs Davenport, it is kind indeed though I am sure I could not drink anything for I can hardly swallow, but I will try and take a sip. I must be better for Jennette's come-out for she cannot go unattended and dear Marcus relies on me . . . he was always such a nice little boy, you know. I used to love to come to Felbeck Abbey to visit . . . and then my poor aunt died and Marcus was left with no brothers and sisters. I think he welcomed me as a playmate even though I was nine years his senior; we rode out together for he had a pony and there was one for me as well . . . I used to ride in those days, but I was younger and not so fearful I suppose. I have my dress all ready for the ball and Jennette's gown is beautiful. It is a pity you cannot be there, sometimes I forget you are the housekeeper. I am afraid Jennette sees too much of Merrick, but he is such a nice boy and so polite to me, I don't like to interfere . . . yes, I will have a sip. Is your gown ready for the ball, Mrs Davenport? It will be a glittering occasion . . . I feel sleepy, you know, did you put something in the barley water . . . ?'

Anthea, who had indeed put a few drops of laudanum in the drink, saw thankfully that Miss Craddock was nodding off to sleep. She put the glass on the bedside table and went to go out of the door only to collide with the earl

138

who was coming in.

'What are you doing playing sick nurse?' he said tetchily. 'I suppose I had better get someone in to her. How is she?'

'She is not at all well and it is no bother to me, My Lord,' Anthea replied.

'Yes, but I don't want you catching the wretched illness. Come into the library. I have something to say to you.'

He seemed in an ill-humour and Anthea followed him downstairs wondering what was concerning him. She was soon to find out.

'Sit by the fire, Mrs Davenport, I wish to speak to you. Will you have a glass of ratafia?'

'No thank you, My Lord.'

'I wish you would call me Marcus.'

She was immediately incensed; surely they were not going to argue again. 'How can I call you by your first name, it would be most disrespectful of me?'

He gave a grin then. 'I've made you cross, Anthea, and I have no wish to do that because I must practise my powers of persuasion on you. What are we going to do about Martha?'

'Miss Craddock?' Anthea was quite bewildered.

'Yes, Miss Craddock. I've just met Dr Black and he tells me she will not be well enough to leave the house for a week.'

Anthea nodded. 'Yes, I know. She is still counting on being better for the ball. She is in a fever at the moment and I don't think she realizes that she will not be well enough to attend.'

'So what are we going to do?'

'What do you mean?' She really was at a loss to understand him.

'Come, Mrs Davenport, my dear Anthea, you are not usually slow to grasp these matters. Who will chaperon Jennette at the ball if Martha is unable to come?'

Anthea swallowed hard and was silent. It was true that she had been so concerned at Miss Craddock's illness, she had given the matter no thought. And with a flash of understanding, she knew what the earl was trying to say to her.

'No,' she replied adamantly. 'I am no more fit to go now than I was when we spoke of the matter before. What about Jennette's aunt?'

'There is not the time to go to Sussex and back to fetch her.' He was sitting across from her by the fireplace and he leaned forward in his chair and touched her hand. 'Anthea, don't let me down. You are the ideal person to present Jennette and I will have you announced as Miss Davenport of Loxley Hall and a friend of the family.'

'I am your housekeeper and everyone will know that.'

'You are obstinate,' he shot at her.

'You are unreasonable,' was her reply.

He took her by the hand and his grip was urgent. 'Anthea, I know you are trying to

140

observe the conventions but you must be able to see what a fix we are in. Do it for Jennette's sake. Please, Anthea, do you realize that I am begging you and I never have to plead for something I want as I am doing now.'

'I have no gown,' she said stonily. A part of her knew that she couldn't let Jennette down and yet there was something in her that dreaded being pointed out in the Assembly Rooms as the earl's housekeeper. It is my pride, she said to herself.

'What do you mean, you have no gown?' He was geniunely puzzled.

'I brought only dresses which would suit my position as housekeeper and one decent dress for the church service on Sundays. None of them is suitable for a ball; my gowns are all left behind in Cumberland.'

'Mrs Peacock,' said the earl.

'Mrs Peacock?' echoed Anthea.

'Yes, Mrs Peacock of Spurriergate. She is not only a linen-draper and milliner, she makes gowns of the most fashionable materials from London. You must have heard Jennette talk of going to York to be fitted for a new gown.'

'Yes, of course I have but, My Lord, it is only two days to the ball and no mantua-maker in the world could make a fashionable gown in that time.'

But there was no arguing with the earl in this mood. 'Be ready to come with me to York

141

this afternoon, Mrs Davenport. You can be sure that Mrs Peacock will have just finished a gown for a lady of fashion and that it would fit you. I will pay her handsomely and she can immediately start on a new gown and her customer will never know.'

Anthea laughed then. 'Oh, Marcus, you cannot be so autocratic—' She stopped as she saw his expression. It changed from one of authority to one of sweet tenderness in a second and, too late, she realized why.

He put a finger to her lips. 'My dear girl, you called me by my name and it came quite easily, did it not? Now you can use it again.'

She should have been angry with herself but his tone was so disarming that she gave a rueful reply. 'It just seemed to slip from me; I will remember another time, My Lord.'

He caught hold of her hands and lifted her to her feet. 'You will do just as I say so go about your duties and I will tell Jennette of the change of plan. She will be very pleased not to have poor Martha fussing round her, the little puss.'

Afterwards, Anthea thought she would never forget the day that Samuel-Coachman drove her and the earl to York to purchase her ball gown.

She had never in her life been to a formal public ball, but she had often had gowns made for her by the Carlisle dressmaker for the country house dances she had attended. She was no stranger to fashion.

The earl handed her out of the carriage at the Spurriergate premises of Mrs Peacock and Anthea later thought that what followed had been more like a charade.

Marcus himself was dressed superbly in a blue superfine coat fitting his athletic figure like a glove and worn over white pantaloons and shining Hessians. The glory of his dress was his waistcoat, for Anthea was used to seeing him dress more modestly. It was embroidered in grey and silver and looked to come straight from London or Paris; his shirt points were not excessively high but his neck cloth was impeccable.

Mrs Peacock, the owner of the establishment which she ran with her daughters, knew the earl and this somehow amused Anthea though she later discovered that he had been there with Jennette.

'My Lord,' said the good woman as they entered. 'Your ward is not with you today? I hope she is pleased with her gown; it was a pleasure to make it for such a beautiful young lady.'

'Yes, she is both delighted and excited. We have come to ask your help. This is Miss Davenport from Loxley Hall in Cumberland, she is visiting unexpectedly not knowing we were about to celebrate a family occasion so she brought no gown with her. I have brought her to you because I am sure you must have

143

one finished that would suit her colouring.'

'Oh yes, My Lord, I have just finished a gown for Lady Welburn, but I can hardly let you have that.'

'And why not? Does she need it immediately?' he asked, and again Anthea could not help but notice the autocratic air about him.

'No, no, it is for the race meeting at the end of the month, there is always a ball afterwards, as you know—'

'Good,' the earl interrupted. 'Then you will have time to make another one in its place . . . may we see it, please?'

'Marcus . . .' Anthea felt she must protest. How could she take a gown intended for another?

'Go with Mrs Peacock and try it on, Anthea, and then come and show me and I will tell you if I approve.' He swept her protestations aside.

Anthea followed Mrs Peacock into the fitting-room and when she saw the gown, she gave a gasp. It was of the best lustrous satin and its colour was a pale gold; in design it was deceptively simple, but the bodice was cut daringly low and had an edging of fine lace; the skirt was full and had garlands of flowers along the hem.

'This is the dress, ma'am,' said Mrs Peacock. 'I would suggest that I take off the garland from the skirt and leave it plain. That is more suitable for someone as young as yourself.

144

Then when I make up the new dress for Her Ladyship, I can use them again and she will never know. For yourself, I would suggest a band of plain gold at the waist; I think that is all the ornament you need, for you are very beautiful, if you don't mind me saying. Would you like to try it on, I am sure it will be a good fit?'

The next ten minutes went by in a haze to Anthea. The gown fitted as though it had been made for her and Mrs Peacock quickly snipped the garlands from the hem and fixed a gold band around the high waist.

'Put this shawl around your arms and go and show yourself to the earl, I am sure he will be pleased.'

Anthea had taken a quick look at herself in the cheval looking-glass and had the impression that it was someone else looking back at her. Shyly, she stepped back into the shop where Marcus was seated at the counter.

'Marcus,' she said.

He looked up and rose to his feet. 'My God, Anthea, I always said you were a beauty and this proves it. It is just as though it was made for you.' He turned to the modiste. 'Yes, Mrs Peacock, we will take it if you would kindly put it in a box and have it taken out to my carriage . . . long gloves? Yes, we will purchase them while we are here. Thank you very much. Go out to the carriage, Anthea, while I settle matters with Mrs Peacock.'

145

Anthea found herself seated once again in the carriage and feeling as Cinderella must have felt after the visit of the Fairy Godmother, she thought to herself with rather a pleased smile. In minutes, Marcus was at her side and smiling at her.

'Now you can hold your head high,' he told her and did not let her know of his immense satisfaction at seeing her so beautifully dressed.

'Thank you very much, My Lord.'

'Marcus.'

'Thank you, Marcus,' she said primly.

*   *   *

On the night of the ball, the Felbeck Abbey party arrived at the Assembly Rooms in good time so that they could greet their guests and make the introductions.

Jennette looked enchanting in the customary white, a very simple gown with lace let into the bodice and the same pattern of lace gathered round the hem. Her fair curls framed her face and one or two ringlets were allowed to drop to her shoulders; she had pearls round her neck and threaded through her hair.

Merrick, looking handsome in pale grey and mauve was at her side, but Jennette had her hand through the arm of her guardian. Behind them walked Anthea, feeling confidently

146

beautiful and correct for the occasion. She entered with Mr and Mrs Downes who made up the party together with their niece Phoebe. She was a tall, slim girl and as soon as they were inside the rooms, she attached herself to Stephen.

Some of the older guests went immediately to the Round Room for cards and the younger members of the company waited for the orchestra to start the music for the first country dance.

The Felbeck Abbey party sat together on the wooden bench which ran around the whole of the ball-room in front of the magnificent pillars. As the first dance started to form, Anthea felt Marcus make a movement to lead Jennette into the set. Then she gasped and at the same time, she felt the earl stiffen.

For Jennette, who should have taken her guardian as her first partner, was to be seen chattering happily to Merrick as they headed the set.

'Marcus,' said Anthea; she did not know what to do.

'Be quiet,' he snapped back. 'Pretend nothing has happened, the naughty girl. I told her she was to take me as her partner for the first dance and to dance no more than three dances with Merrick. Anthea, stand up with me as though you are proud to be with me and no one will notice that Jennette has behaved improperly.'

CHAPTER EIGHT

Anthea had ample opportunity for speaking to Marcus while the other dancers made their way down the set, but she hardly knew what to say. She was aware of his displeasure at Jennette's behaviour and wondered, not for the first time, how ever the ill-assorted pair would fare as man and wife.

The sight of Stephen and Phoebe Downes dancing very well together gave her an opening. 'Look, Marcus, Stephen and Phoebe seem a very nice pair, they are both tall and fair and appear to be getting along famously. Has Stephen met Phoebe before?'

'Yes, many times. So do you think Phoebe would do for Stephen then?' he asked her.

Anthea's reply came before she really thought about what she was saying and to whom she was addressing. 'No, I don't, I think it is Jennette who would do for Stephen.'

He glanced at her and did not look best pleased. 'What are you talking about? I intend to announce my betrothal to Jennette on her birthday.'

Anthea knew she had spoken out of turn and tried to make up for her hasty remark. 'I do know that and I wish you happiness.' But the words came automatically and not from the heart.

'You sound waspish, what is the matter?' he asked.

'Worrying about Jennette, I suppose, going off with Merrick like that when she knew very well she should have opened her ball with you. It is not usually my responsibility, but it is tonight and I have a feeling that your ward is going to make a fool of herself over Merrick.'

'You *are* in an odd mood and you are supposed to be my radiant partner to let everyone know that I do not care that Jennette has misbehaved. Dance the first waltz with me and I will whisk your cares away.'

'I don't dance the waltz.'

'I will teach you.'

'No doubt you are an expert.'

'Yes, I am, you only have to follow me.'

Anthea had to smile. She would have followed him anywhere, she thought. 'The set is coming to a close, are you going to speak to Jennette?'

'I don't want to spoil her evening but I suppose I shall have to say something.'

Marcus led her to their seats and Jennette came up smiling and happy. 'Isn't it all lovely,' she said.

Marcus looked at her. 'You were supposed to open the ball with me, Jennette.'

She looked crestfallen but not in the least penitent. 'Oh, Marcus, so I was, for you told me so, but Merrick asked me first and I couldn't refuse him, could I? Shall I dance the waltz with you?'

'I am dancing the waltz with Anthea,' he replied.

Jennette smiled happily. 'Oh good, that means I can dance it with Merrick and I will save the last dance for him for I do remember that I am allowed only three dances with the same gentleman. That is proper. Do you know, my card is full already, I am going to be a success.'

Anthea met Marcus's eyes across the young girl's head and they were both laughing. What else was there to do?

'Hussy,' said one pair of eyes.

'Minx,' said the other.

But the evening proved a successful and glittering occasion and it appeared to be the general opinion that Jennette and Merrick Downes were well suited and that the Earl of Felbeck had met his match in the good-looking visitor from Cumberland.

*   *   *

Jennette was soon to receive many invitations and was once again accompanied by the now-recovered Miss Craddock.

Phoebe still visited at Downes Hall and she and Jennette soon became bosom-bows, going everywhere together. Jennette even allowed Phoebe to accompany herself and Merrick on

150

their morning rides.

Then two days before they were due to go in a party to the Spring Race Meeting on the Knavesmire in York and to the ball afterwards, Merrick asked the earl for his permission to address himself to Jennette.

Merrick had arrived that morning to seek his interview with Marcus and, for once, was not dressed for riding. He was wearing a great coat with several capes and was driving his own curricle.

The earl received Merrick in the library and having already noticed that Jennette had the fidgets, he could guess the purpose of the young man's visit. He offered his visitor a glass of wine which Merrick politely refused.

'No thank you, Marcus, I would just like a few words with you.'

'Yes, certainly, my boy, I trust you are not in Dun Territory again?'

'No, sir, nothing like that.' Merrick was a handsome boy and could be very charming; he could impress with his seriousness of purpose and tried to do so before the earl now. 'I think you must be aware that Jennette and I have become great friends over the winter, indeed you have been good enough to allow me to ride with her each morning. She is a capital little horsewoman, isn't she?'

'Yes, I think she is, Merrick. Go on.'

Encouraged by the earl's seemingly genial tone, Merrick ploughed into the purpose of

151

the interview. 'Jennette has told me of the promise you made to her father and I know you would wish to honour it. But I love Jennette very much and I believe she loves me sincerely. I cannot be sure if you are willing to break your pledge, but it would please me very much if you would permit me to address myself to Jennette with a view to asking her to become my wife.'

The Earl of Felbeck looked at Merrick who, having known him well all his life, he had always thought to be a rather shallow character, easily swayed by his emotions and too readily influenced by his dandy-set friends in the gaming clubs of York and London.

Marcus had no intention of letting Jennette become the wife of the loose screw who was the youngest member of the very respectable Downes family, but he was curious to know of Merrick's intentions should he receive the permission he sought.

'I have seen that Jennette has a very high regard for you, Merrick,' he said, 'and I am sure that regard is returned. A union between my ward and a member of the Downes family would not be out of the question, but I fail to see what means you have of supporting a wife and family. You will forgive me asking you this but you will understand that it is of the first importance to me as her guardian.'

Merrick was not thrown by the question and remained cool and civil. Marcus felt he had to credit the young man with great aplomb. 'It is true that my allowance is small and I have no profession, but I did not think that to be a consideration as I believe Jennette expects to inherit a considerable fortune.'

'So you are a fortune hunter! I knew I would have to be on the watch as soon as her expectations became known.'

Merrick was as tall as the earl and faced him squarely. 'I do not see myself in that category,' he replied without flinching. 'I have met many young ladies of substance but I have never loved or wanted to marry one of them as I do Jennette.'

'I understand and I am sorry to disappoint you. It is my intention to keep my promise to Jennette's father and to marry my ward as soon as I consider she is ready to take up the reins of Felbeck Abbey. It is my wish to let her have a season before I tie her down to family life. That is all, Merrick, and I wish you good day and hope we will remain friends. I am sure Jennette will be disappointed but I expect her to obey my wishes.'

Merrick stood by the door. 'It is not the end of it, Marcus; we will let Jennette have her season in York and then I will approach you again. Good day.'

Marcus watched the young man from the library window and saw him get into his curricle and drive off; he thought the flick of the young man's whip was angry and he sat down thoughtfully. He is after Jennette's money, I am sure of it, he said to himself. She might imagine she is in love with Merrick but he has flattered her into thinking that theirs is a lasting passion. I may not wish to marry her myself at this very moment but neither do I want to see her married to the like of the Merrick Downes of this world.

He went in search of his ward and discovered her to be riding with Phoebe, then as he had business in York and dined there, he did not see her until the next day.

Jennette had gone off anxiously that morning to meet Merrick and Phoebe knowing that Merrick would have seen her guardian on the previous day and wondering what the outcome had been.

In Phoebe's presence, Merrick could say little but as they were to meet up at Home Wood, he rode ahead and brought his horse close to Jennette and reached out for her hand. He seemed gloomy.

'It is all up with us, Jennette, your guardian is determined to marry you. But don't worry your pretty little head, I will think of something.'

'Oh, Merrick, I had a feeling that would be the answer. What will we do? I refuse to give you up.'

'Leave it to me; we cannot say more for Phoebe is riding up. I got ahead of her so that I could exchange a few words with you;

promise you won't fret, we'll come about.' He lifted her gloved hand and kissed the palm. 'I love you.'

'Oh, Merrick.'

On Jennette's return, the first person she saw at Felbeck Abbey was Stephen as he returned from the stables. 'Wait for me, Stephen,' she called out. 'I'll just hand Tessa over to Jed. She needs a rub-down; I came home rather fast.'

Stephen waited at the door of the stables and they walked slowly back to the house together, pausing at the group of laurels near the front door.

'Stephen, do you think Marcus will marry me?' she blurted out.

Stephen was used to Jennette's ways but even this sudden question startled him. 'I don't know what my cousin's intentions are, I only know of his promise to your father.'

She looked up at him. She felt confident and sure when she was with Stephen for he always listened to her and his words never failed to put her in the right direction. She had often thought that if she hadn't fallen in love with Merrick, it would have been Stephen she would have chosen as a husband and not her guardian.

'He has told Merrick we cannot marry. I love Merrick so much, Stephen. I love you, too, but in a different kind of way. But you wouldn't wish me to be unhappy, would you,

Stephen?'

I'd better go carefully, thought Stephen, Marcus must have his reasons for turning Merrick down though I cannot believe that he wants to marry Jennette himself. Every day I think it is Anthea he leans towards; that would be a more suitable match even if she is his housekeeper at the moment. Stephen had often looked into his own heart and had found that there was only one woman in the world for him and she was this beautiful little scamp who trusted him so much. She was gazing up at him now, blue eyes anxious and with a little frown.

'Your happiness is very important to me,' he answered quite truthfully. 'Perhaps Marcus thinks that you and Merrick are rather young; why not see your season out and then Merrick can approach Marcus again.'

Her brow cleared as if by magic. 'Yes, you are right, there is no rush and we are not going to stop loving one another just because Marcus has said no the first time. Dear Stephen, what would I do without you? It is the race meeting tomorrow and I've never been to one before. It is all too exciting to be worried just because Marcus has refused Merrick permission to address me.' She took his arm and they entered the house. 'It is time for a nuncheon, Stephen.'

They all sat round the breakfast table for their cold meat and ale and Jennette thought that Marcus seemed to be in a stern mood. Miss Craddock would talk of nothing but the races.

'Marcus,' she said. 'I have never been to a race meeting, I have no interest in horses and I do not approve of gambling. I really would rather not go to York tomorrow; could you not take Mrs Davenport as you did to Jennette's ball? I am sure she would like to go; she was probably used to going to race meetings in Cumberland.'

The earl eyed her wearily and he seemed to have something else on his mind as he replied rather absent-mindedly, 'Yes, Martha, you need not come if you have no wish to. I will ask Anthea.'

If Miss Craddock was surprised that he had called his housekeeper by her forename, she did not say so; but Stephen did notice and it gave him a little feeling of satisfaction as he wondered if he was right and that the wind was blowing that way.

Jennette was pleased, too. 'I would like Mrs Davenport to come, I am sure you would not enjoy it, Miss Craddock.'

As they got up from the table, the earl put his hand on Jennette's shoulder. 'Come into the library, Jennette, I would like a word with you in private.'

Jennette could guess what that private word would be and was prepared to do battle to win Merrick.

They sat together on a long, leather sofa and Marcus looked down at his ward; she had changed from her riding clothes into a dress of white muslin, embroidered with tiny blue flowers; the sleeves were puffed; the neck was low even for the daytime and her golden curls were not worn high but loose about her head and gathered together in a single band.

I suppose she is beautiful, he sighed; I cannot blame Merrick for falling in love with her or with her money, whichever is the more correct. And Stephen can hardly keep his eyes from her these days but I suppose he is too old for her; I am too old for her, as well, but I will not release her to a puppy like Merrick Downes.

Jennette gazed up at him and he could not help but be amused because she had the impudence to look innocent.

'What is it, Marcus? Do you think Miss Craddock should come with us tomorrow? I am sure I would rather have Mrs Davenport.'

'Your sentiment does you no credit, Jennette. Martha may be a rattle-pate but she is a good woman and has looked after you properly.' He paused. 'What is all this about Merrick Downes?'

'Merrick? What do you mean? I've been riding with him and Phoebe today, you know.'

'Don't play the innocent, you know very well that Merrick sought an interview with me yesterday.'

'And you turned him down, Marcus. Why did you do that? He is of a good family and the Downes are very respectable.' Jennette's eyes did not waver.

'Their youngest son is not respectable. He is of the dandy-set and is addicted to gaming. His sort do not usually look to marriage so young when they are on the town. I can think of only one reason for him wanting to marry you. I believe him to be on the rocks again, his father refuses to fund him and he looks to your fortune.'

'Marcus.' Jennette raised her voice for the first time. 'It simply is not true. Merrick loves me and has shown me so in many ways and I love him. I don't mind waiting for him if only you will give your permission.'

'Never, Jennette. I've no doubt that Merrick has flattered you with his intentions, his compliments and his kisses, which you should have known better than to accept. I will not give my consent to you becoming his wife and that is my final word.'

'It is not my final word.' Jennette jumped up like a little spitfire.

'Jennette, your manners,' her guardian thundered. 'I promised to marry you and I intend to keep that promise, though God knows I don't deserve such a fate as to be married to a spoiled little baggage like you. Yes, I know that is impolite but I am not feeling polite. You will not marry Merrick.'

159

Jennette stamped her feet. 'And I will not marry you. I don't love you and I don't think we should suit. I would rather be married to Stephen, at least he is kind to me.'

'Marry Stephen then.' Marcus had lost his temper by now.

Jennette glared at him. 'So you would forget your promise for Stephen, would you? But not for Merrick. I will wait for Merrick and he will wait for me, I know he will. It is only two years until I am in control of my fortune and we will wait.'

'Just you see if Merrick will wait, my girl. I will be very surprised if he does. In any case, I will have secured you as my wife by that time.'

'Never . . .' Jennette cried out, burst into tears and ran from the room.

The Earl of Felbeck went in search of his housekeeper; he knew he should not but he also knew that she was the only person who would calm his frayed temper. I didn't handle that very well, he was saying to himself. What on earth would it be like to be married to the little shrew?

He found Anthea, not in her sitting-room but walking through the garden admiring the buds on the first roses.

'Walk with me to the ruins,' he said abruptly and on the verge of rudeness.

Anthea looked at him astonished. 'Whatever has happened to put you out of humour, My Lord?'

160

'I am not out of humour, I am in a bad temper and my ward has caused it. And I am not "My Lord", I am Marcus.'

'Oh, Marcus, for goodness' sake, not that again—there, I have called you by your name. We'd better sit on the stones in the corner of the ruins and you can tell what has caused you to be upset.'

It being the third week in May and the sun shining from a clear sky, Anthea was dressed in a simple cotton dress of pale green; true it was high to the neck but so was the waist high and showed her splendid figure to advantage. She carried no shawl and her hair was piled high.

She looks majestic, the earl thought. What a difference from this flibbertigibbet ward of mine. I could lay my head on Anthea's breast and feel both comfort and excitement. But he took himself to task. I haven't come here to think such thoughts, he remonstrated with himself.

They sat on the same stones that had seen them exchange passionate kisses; Marcus looked at Anthea and made himself forget.

'Now what is it?' she said in an even tone.

'Jennette says she wants to marry Merrick and is prepared to wait for him forever. I think he's up to no good and I have refused him permission to address her.'

She looked at him curiously. 'You think the same then? I told Stephen that I didn't trust

161

Merrick but Stephen was inclined to think that he was just a young rascal and no real harm in him. Jennette has certainly been much better behaved since she has known Merrick, none of the tantrums I thought we were going to have to endure.'

'I've endured one today.'

'Oh dear, did you tell her she couldn't marry Merrick?'

'I did.'

'And she didn't like it?'

'No. She didn't like the idea of being married to me either.'

'You are going to marry her then?' Anthea did not know that it was said sadly.

He looked at her. 'Do you mind?'

She smiled at the question. 'My Lord, it is not for the housekeeper to mind who her employer chooses to marry. I think Jennette will be very fortunate to become the Countess of Felbeck.'

'I think she would rather be Mrs Merrick Downes,' he said ruefully.

'She is a foolish child,' Anthea replied.

'Child is the appropriate word for she is still a child to me. I cannot think of her as a wife, Anthea. There, I've been honest.'

Anthea's heart had plummeted at the thought of Jennette becoming the earl's wife but she knew she had to face up to the fact; she knew of her own love for Marcus but she had never let it be shown and she

162

wouldn't now.

'You are going to keep your promise to her father?' she asked. He nodded. 'I must unless someone more suitable comes along to offer for Jennette. And it certainly won't be Merrick Downes.' He turned towards her and put his hand to her waist. 'This is where we kiss, Anthea.'

'Not today, Marcus.'

'Thank you for the Marcus. I will take my kiss.'

And she was in his arms, her head forced back with the strength of his lips on hers. Passion was between them once again and neither wanted the moment to end. Finally Anthea's face was wet with tears and love as she lay against his chest.

'You have everything my ward has not and I cannot have you,' he said harshly. 'Go back to your duties, go back to Stephen and see if he will have you, although I've a feeling he has eyes for no one but Jennette. What a coil.'

And he jumped up and strode off in the direction of his cherished house. Anthea watched him go, her body still throbbing, her heart still aching.

She sat there for what seemed a long time, eyes shut and dreaming of things that could never be. She opened them to the sound of her name being softly said.

'Anthea.'

She looked up in astonishment to see

Stephen standing there. And she smiled for they were good friends. 'How did you know I was here?' she asked him.

'I met Marcus just coming into the house in a tearing hurry and he told me to come and find you here and that you needed comfort.'

She frowned. 'What an extraordinary thing to say.'

'What did he mean?'

'I'm not sure,' she said, but she wondered if Marcus had read more into her feelings than she had meant him to know. 'We have just been talking about Jennette.'

'And he said he is bound to marry her and he refuses to let her marry Merrick,' he said.

She nodded and gave a wan smile. 'Has she been talking to you? I gather she didn't behave herself very well when Marcus told her what had been said to Merrick.'

'Naughty puss.' Stephen smiled indulgently. 'She really believes herself to be in love with Merrick. I told her to wait until the end of the season, enjoy herself and then perhaps Merrick could ask Marcus again.'

'Sensible Stephen, she will listen to you, won't she? I think you are the only one with any influence over her. But Marcus isn't going to change his mind, is he? He told me so.'

'No, I don't think he will. That promise to his dying friend is a very serious matter to him.' He sat on the stones beside her and took her hand in his. 'I must ask you, would you marry me, Anthea?'

She looked at him with great fondness in her eyes. 'Thank you for asking me, Stephen, but the answer must be no. You see, I don't love you as I like to think I will love the man I might marry . . .' She paused, not sure whether to pursue the subject. 'In any case, you are in love with Jennette, are you not?'

He looked sad. 'Yes, I think I loved her the moment I first saw her for all she turned out to be a wayward little miss. But my case is hopeless, is it not? Jennette imagines herself to be in love with Merrick and is supposed to be promised to Marcus though somehow I can't see that match ever coming off in spite of what he says.' He tightened his hold on her hand. 'And what about you, my Anthea, I sometimes think it is Marcus you love? I can see that look in your eyes.'

Anthea was honest with him for it seemed to be a time for straight speaking. 'I'm not sure, Stephen, sometimes I feel as though there is no one else in the world for me but Marcus, but then Jennette gets in the way and I am jealous.'

Stephen gave a chuckle. 'I think that is true love, Anthea. I wonder what our destiny will bring the two of us, both of us with a hopeless love. We can remain friends, I am sure of that.'

She nodded and smiled gently. 'Yes, I would like to remain friends, Stephen, I feel I can always turn to you.'

165

'I am here, my Anthea.' He leaned forward and kissed her lips and she liked the gesture for it seemed almost brotherly and it was what she needed.

*   *   *

The next day found two carriages from Skelton making the journey to the York Knavesmire and the Spring Race Meeting which began on 30 May that year.

Before the Felbeck Abbey carriage had set off there had been the usual argument between the earl and his housekeeper. Anthea had known that Miss Craddock disapproved of racing but had thought that Jennette would be sufficiently chaperoned as Mrs Downes and Phoebe would be in the party.

After breakfast, Marcus had sought Anthea out. She was in the kitchen talking over the dinner menu with Sarah. He called to her from the door. 'Anthea, are you not getting ready? There is only an hour, you know.'

She left Sarah and went up to him. 'I am not going to the races, My Lord,' she said.

'Come into my study.' He could not argue with her in front of their cook. Anthea followed and was prepared for trouble; she would very much like to have gone to the races and for almost the first time, she regretted her position.

'Anthea, I could not argue with you in front

of Sarah. You are coming to the races. Jennette needs a stronger hand than Phoebe's and I cannot expect or wish for Mrs Downes to feel responsible for her. It would be assuming a familiarity I would prefer to avoid at the moment.'

'Marcus, you know it is not proper for me to go. You will end up with a scandal on your hands.'

'Rubbish,' he said with acerbity. 'There was no scandal after the ball and I wish you to come. Does that not weigh with you?'

She softened. 'I would like to go, I used to enjoy the racing at Kingsmoor in Carlisle, but I still hesitate.'

'It would please me and it would benefit Jennette, can I say more?'

His hand was on her shoulder and his fingers stroked the skin at the neck of her dress. It was a tiny caress but it was one of persuasion and caring and Anthea gave in.

'I will say yes, then.' And, she added almost impishly, 'To please you.'

'Bless you; off you go and get changed out of your uniform.'

'It is *not* my uniform . . .' she started to say and knew she had capitulated to his teasing.

'You know what I mean . . . but give me a kiss first, I can hardly kiss you at the races.'

And before she had time to think let alone protest, he had pulled her hard against him and found her lips in a persuasive kiss that she

167

could not resist.

'Marcus . . .' But the protest was too late for he was laughing with a delight she had never seen in him before.

'Thank you, Anthea, that was very nice. I will see you at the front door in an hour.'

And so the two carriages set off, the one from Downes Hall with Mr and Mrs Downes, Merrick and Phoebe; and the one from Felbeck Abbey carrying the earl and Stephen with Anthea and an excited Jennette. The young girl was dressed in deep gold, as a change from the usual blue, and looked very stylish; her high bonnet was adorned with flowers the same colour as her dress.

The great stand at the Knavesmire was a hub of activity and the Skelton party were soon arguing over which horse they should back in the first race.

Marcus and Stephen were all for Lord Fitzwilliam's bay colt, Dinmont, but the girls disagreed.

'I think Fulford is a better horse because it has a York name,' announced Phoebe, and Jennette agreed with her.

But Merrick scoffed at them. 'That's typical of a girl,' he said. 'Choosing a winner because of its name. I am sure Lord Scarborough's Hurricane is the best bet, it's a chestnut colt and I fancy it.'

So the earl went off to place the bets and the excitement grew. By the time they realized that Fulford was going to win, with Dinmont and Hurricane second and third, Anthea—who had lost her money on Hurricane—looked round and found that Jennette was missing from the party.

'Where is Jennette?' she asked.

She was met with blank looks from the others and then, to their consternation, they found that Merrick was missing, as well.

CHAPTER NINE

While the others in the party were keenly watching the race, Merrick, who was standing by Jennette, took her arm urgently and whispered so that only she could hear.

'Jennette, I must speak with you, let's slip off to the wood where it will be private.'

The Knavesmire wood was on the edge of the racecourse and some distance away. Jennette protested.

'But it is too far, Merrick.'

But he was already urging her away from their party and Jennette followed. 'It will only take us five minutes to get there and no one will see us in this crowd. I must speak to you, Jennette.'

With a sense that she should not be going off on her own but unable to withstand Merrick's wishes, Jennette walked quickly at his side until they reached the dense trees of the wood.

He drew her into a spot where the trees were thickest and stood her with her back against a solid tree trunk.

His fingers touched her cheek, her throat and strayed to the softness of her high breasts in her fashionable gown. 'My God, Jennette, you are beautiful. I've never seen anyone to touch you for beauty. I love you so much and I am determined to have you.' His lips followed where his fingers had been and Jennette felt both excitement and unease. She knew she should not allow him such liberties but she was flattered by his attentions, his touch and his love. 'I told you that Marcus has refused me permission to address you,' he said quietly.

She nodded. 'Yes, I am sorry, he is determined to keep his promise to my papa. What shall we do, Merrick?'

'Do you truly love me?' Merrick took her into his arms. His kiss was sensuous and he urged her body towards him.

Jennette was torn in two. She knew she should not allow such intimate behaviour, but her body cried out with love for the young man.

'Yes, I do love you . . .' she gasped, as his lips sought her. 'Oh, Merrick . . .

'And you do want to marry me?'

'More than anything in the world,' she replied.

'And would you marry me if we ran off together to be wed?'

His fingers were caressing the curve of her breast and Jennette's last notion of propriety vanished; she cried out in excitement, 'An elopement? Oh, Merrick, could we do it? Do you mean for us to go to Gretna Green? Would you really marry me? What an adventure it would be.'

And she threw her arms round his neck, losing any sense of decorum at the thought of being Merrick's wife.

Merrick kissed her gladly and then was careful in his choice of words. 'You are a wonderful girl and I love you very much. Are you willing to leave all the arrangements to me and to be ready with just a bag packed when I tell you?'

Jennette agreed eagerly but had a sudden thought. 'But what would we do for money, Merrick?'

He laughed. 'Don't you worry your pretty little head about that. I have enough for the journey and when we return as man and wife, Marcus is sure to advance you some of your money for us to live on.' He felt her stiffen and hesitate and stopped her doubts with another long kiss. 'Marcus has always been a good friend to me and I have the feeling he doesn't really want to marry you himself.'

Jennette looked at him. 'Do you really think so, Merrick? I have often wondered, he seems to have a *tendre* for Mrs Davenport, doesn't he? I know she is only his housekeeper but she is of a good family.'

'I am sure so. He will be pleased I have taken you off his hands,' Marcus replied easily.

'Then why did he refuse you?'

'I think he genuinely thought you should have your first season. He is also a man of honour and would wish to keep any promise he had made.' Merrick was still holding her close and she was as light as thistledown in his arms.

Jennette could only agree. 'I think you are right. How long will it take you to make the arrangements for our elopement? Oh, I am so excited at the thought. It is like a story book.'

'I think a trip to Scarborough is planned for the day after tomorrow,' he told her seriously. 'I will tell you then. And now I think we should be getting back or they will all be wondering where we are.'

Marcus and Stephen had indeed been searching for the missing pair and when they came walking along the racecourse with Jennette unable to hide her excitement, Marcus lost his temper with her.

'Jennette, it was most improper of you to go off on your own with Merrick. In future you stay at Mrs Davenport's side. I am sorry to say that I do not trust you.'

But Jennette was unrepentant and reached up and kissed her guardian on the cheek.

'Don't be cross, Marcus. Merrick and I only walked as far as the wood and we have come straight back. I suppose it was wrong of me not to take a chaperon, but I am so used to Merrick now and I have come to no harm.'

He looked down at her. She looked particularly enchanting and after all, he said to himself, she is no more than a child. I don't suppose there was any harm in a stroll to the wood to seek an innocent kiss. So he tried to laugh off his censure.

'You are a naughty puss and it's no wonder Merrick has fallen in love with you. I expect the two of you have been discussing my refusal to countenance a marriage when you are so young, but you won't make me change my mind, however sweetly you behave to me.' He turned round and beckoned to Anthea who had been watching the scene and Jennette's winning ways. 'Here is your charge, Mrs Davenport, don't let her stray again.'

Jennette's behaviour was beyond reproach after that. She danced the waltz with Marcus at the ball after the race meeting and treated Merrick like a beloved brother. Anthea watched suspiciously and mentioned her doubts to Stephen when they stood up for a country dance.

'Stephen, have you seen Jennette?'

'Of course I have seen Jennette, what do you mean?' His tone was amused.

'I mean her behaviour, I am sure she is up

173

to something. She is being particularly charming to Marcus and that is just not like her,' Anthea said, but Stephen only laughed.

'You are jealous because he didn't dance the waltz with you, Anthea,' he teased her.

'Stephen! That is unfair for you know I have no claim on Marcus. I suppose Jennette can do no wrong in your eyes.'

'She does seem very high-spirited today but I think she is enjoying herself and I admit to her being vain. She loves all the attention she is getting. Why are you worrying about her, Anthea?'

Anthea shook her head. 'I really don't know. Since she was reproved by Marcus for disappearing with Merrick at the races, she has been as good as gold and charms everyone. But I seem to detect an air of hidden mischief in her eyes as though she is up to no good! I can't explain it and I expect I am being foolish.'

'You are never foolish, my Anthea.'

'You don't know me, Stephen,' she replied.

'What I do know, I like,' he said. 'Come, it is our turn to go down the set.'

On the day of the planned expedition to Scarborough, once again Anthea was called upon to act as duenna to Jennette.

Miss Craddock sought out Marcus when she should have been getting dressed for the journey. 'Marcus, I really do not like the sea air, I am sure it does not agree with me. I

174

know it would be beneficial to take the waters at the spa but I had rather do that at Harrogate. I would be very grateful if you would excuse me and ask Mrs Davenport to go. She is very good-natured and I think she understands Jennette better than I do. It will be nice for her to have a day at the seaside, I am sure you will agree, for she is very conscientious in her duties and—'

Marcus, pleased at the idea, cut his cousin short with no apology. 'It is kind of you, Martha. I will go and find Mrs Davenport and tell her.' And, as he went off, he said to himself that he would try and arrange the party so that he had his housekeeper to himself.

It was a full coachload, but as it was an occasion for fun, no one minded being crowded into the Felbeck carriage.

Jennette sat with Merrick and Phoebe and Anthea, delighted to be asked to join the expedition, found herself sitting close between Marcus and Stephen.

Samuel-Coachman had two horses up front and, as the road from York to Scarborough was a good one, the journey was a accomplished in record time. They put up at the Talbot Inn in Queen Street and a nuncheon was ordered; then they set off on foot for St Nicholas Cliff where they were afforded a splendid view of the sands, the harbour and the ruins of the castle towering above the sea.

Jennette and Phoebe were watching the young ladies emerging from the wooden bathing machines on the sands.

Jennette gave a laugh as she imagined them shivering. 'It is too cold for me, Phoebe, what do you think?'

Phoebe was inclined to agree. 'The bathers seem to be wearing long thick dresses, I supose their proper clothes are left in the bathing machine. And look at the women helping them get into the water—they've got on long coats and hats and scarves, to keep them warm, I suppose. I've been to Scarborough before but I've never been in the sea. I expect I'm a coward!'

'So am I,' said Jennette. 'I would rather have a horse ride along the sands, would you come with me?'

'Yes, of course I would,' replied the willing Phoebe.

The gentlemen had been looking through the telescopes from the top of the cliff and were appealed to.

Marcus was watching Anthea who looked striking in a morning dress of dull red worn with a short spencer made of a woollen cloth in a darker colour. And he decided to try and keep Anthea for himself; he was out of patience with his ward and she had companions enough.

'Jennette,' he suggested, 'you and Phoebe

176

take horses along the sands with Stephen and Merrick and I will walk with Mrs Davenport into North Bay which I haven't seen for a long time.'

If Anthea was amused by this arrangement on her behalf, she said nothing. She knew that Jennette would come to no harm with Stephen.

So the earl and his housekeeper stood and watched as the other four walked down the steep slope of the cliff to procure horses for themselves, then Marcus gave Anthea his arm.

Anthea,' he said, looking pleased, 'I think I organized that rather nicely, but will you promise me one thing?'

Anthea looked up at the handsome face, expecting laughter but he was quite serious. 'What is that?' she asked him.

'That whatever we do or wherever we go in Scarborough, you will call me Marcus.'

She did laugh then and gave in easily. 'Very well, Marcus, I feel quite light-hearted, it must be the sea air. Do you realize that I have never seen the sea before?'

'I hope you are not disappointed. Would you rather walk up to the castle or round into North Bay, which is quite wild for the town ends at the castle.'

'Oh, the North Bay, I think, it sounds exhilarating.'

They set off at a brisk pace down Cross Street and Auborough and were soon at

North Bay.

'It's lovely,' exclaimed Anthea as they came out of the houses and she saw the stretch of bay before her with its sands and small rock pools waiting to be covered by the incoming waves.

'I thought you would like it. Do you mind walking on the sand, are you suitably shod?'

'Of course I am,' she answered indignantly. 'I would hardly have worn soft kid for a visit to the sea.'

'Good, would you like to walk to the edge of the sea? I think the tide must be on the turn. Give me your hand.'

Anthea put her hand into his and they walked slowly over the firm sand; the wild bay was deserted for most visitors to the town preferred to be near the spa. She had a feeling of great contentment and wondered how long it would last for it seemed almost a stolen moment.

'I feel like a naughty child who has been excused lessons,' she said happily.

'You don't look like a child at all, you look beautiful.'

'Not that again!' she groaned.

'One day I will convince you of your beauty. For the time being, let me take your bonnet off. You must feel the sea breeze in your hair.' He put his fingers to the ribbons.

'It is most unseemly,' she said but she smiled.

'No one is here to notice and in any case, I

178

feel carefree today. I could waltz all along the sands with you; perhaps I will kiss you.'

Anthea looked at him and her heart turned over. Always handsome, today he had a devil-may-care look about him, his mouth was set in a smile, his hair blown by the wind. I will steal this hour from Jennette, she said to herself; Jennette is with her love and I am with mine even if he does not know it. But she had to pretend her indifference.

'You should save your kisses for Jennette,' she told him.

'Bah! Don't spoil things. I am succeeding in forgetting the wretched child for an hour at least.'

She was curious. 'If you feel like that, why do you insist on marrying her? Apart from your promise to her father, that is. You could even have given your permission to Merrick.'

He stopped walking and turned her to face him. 'I feel I would be letting Charles down if I let her marry Merrick. I am certain he would not have approved of the boy or the match. And I must marry to secure the line, so it might as well be Jennette; she is decorative enough and she will probably improve.'

Their eyes met. 'That is hardly the way to speak of a future wife,' Anthea said quietly.

'And what have you to say to the matter?'

'I am not your servant today, I am Anthea and I think I have a wish to see you happy.'

'That is kind of you.'

179

'I am kind.'

'Are you kind enough to allow me a kiss?'

'That is a different matter,' she said, but her tone was still in their mood of light-hearted bantering with each other.

He drew her towards him and she could not resist. 'We cannot come to the seaside without a kiss,' he said, and he put a hand behind her head and guided her lips to his.

The seagulls cried and shrieked overhead, the waves crept closer with a steady roar but the earl and his housekeeper did not notice. Their feelings were heightened in the clear atmosphere of the sea air and they did not want to break apart. Anthea knew she was showing the love she had for this man who was beyond her reach, but for a moment in time she allowed it to be released.

'Anthea, I . . .' His voice was hoarse with emotion.

'I think our feet are getting wet, My Lord.'

And he burst out laughing as he pulled her quickly from the encroaching tide. 'You wretch. Making me think you must love me and then reminding me that you are my housekeeper. And we are behaving like children, stealing kisses on the seashore. We will walk back to sanity and to Jennette and Merrick and leave our feelings and desires behind us in North Bay.'

Anthea was able to laugh, too, and, with damp feet, they hurried back to join the rest of the party who were getting off their horses at the foot of St Nicholas Cliff.

Jennette was both excited and seemingly agitated though Anthea was at a loss to understand why.

'We had a grand time, Mrs Davenport, though the horses were old nags really—mine was called Prince which was a ridiculous name for such a sorry steed. We all rode together to begin with then Merrick and I had a race, though you can't gallop very fast on the sand, you know. We went beyond the Spaw House and Phoebe wanted to try the waters but none of us would go in so we didn't. I hope you had a good walk, did you go as far as the castle?'

And the girl chattered like this all the way back to York while Merrick seemed quiet and Phoebe was preoccupied about something.

The next morning, Jennette was disappointed when only Phoebe arrived for their morning ride; Merrick had sent a message to say that he had gone into York on a business matter. But the two girls went off quite happily leaving Anthea to go about her duties; she had seen neither the earl nor Stephen that morning and had assumed that they, too, had gone off on business.

In the middle of the morning, she was busy at the accounts in her room when she heard a shriek, a cry of distress coming from the direction of the drawing-room.

She rushed out to find Miss Craddock

standing at the drawing-room door looking very upset and alarmed.

'The painting, Mrs Davenport, the painting has gone . . .

'Which painting, Miss Craddock?'

'The family painting, of course, the Van Dyck which always hangs above the fireplace . . . it is not there . . . just a space. Oh, I suppose you could have taken it down for cleaning, yes, that must be it. Do tell me you have taken it for cleaning, Mrs Davenport, or I will think we have been robbed . . .'

Anthea took the hysterical woman by the arm and led her back into the drawing-room where she found that Miss Craddock was indeed right: the family portrait was missing.

'I haven't taken it down for cleaning, Miss Craddock, but the earl may have, or even Mr Lorimer. Do not upset yourself before we have asked them about it, I am sure there must be a satisfactory explanation.' She turned as she heard a noise at the front door. 'Perhaps this is the earl now, let us go and see . . . no, that is Jennette. I can tell by her light step. We had better ask her in case she knows anything.'

Anthea and Miss Craddock went out of the drawing-room to find Jennette about to go up the stairs. As usual, she was in her blue riding habit with the latest in back velvet riding hats, worn at a tilt and showing her fair curls to advantage.

'Jennette,' called Anthea. 'The family

portrait from the drawing-room is missing. Do you know anything about it?'

Anthea thought she detected a hesitation of the briefest of seconds before Jennette replied, but when the girl did speak, it was with her usual vigour and eagerness. 'Oh no, Mrs Davenport, I've no idea where it is if it is not above the fireplace. Marcus has probably arranged to have it cleaned for it was very dark, you know, probably from the smoke of the fire.'

As Anthea thought this to be a sensible suggestion, she let Jennette proceed upstairs and then turned back to Miss Craddock. 'I think Jennette is probably right, she is not usually so discerning. So do stop worrying and we will wait until the earl comes home. I think he must have gone over to one of the farms with Mr Lorimer.'

'Yes, I believe he has, Mrs Davenport; I knew I could rely on you and I expect you are right. But when you notice something like that, the immediate thought must be that there has been a robbery. And of course, the Van Dyck is valuable. Do you think, Mrs Davenport, that it might be a good idea for us to have a look round to make sure that nothing else is missing?'

For once, Anthea credited the fussy little woman with good sense and the two of them made a thorough search of the house but found nothing missing. James, the footman, assisted them for he had been employed in the house for many years and knew each piece of furniture and the pottery and porcelain in every detail. But he found nothing amiss and was inclined to the same view as Miss Craddock and thought that the earl must have taken it to York to be cleaned.

But when Marcus and Stephen arrived home for a very late nuncheon, neither of them had any knowledge of the whereabouts of the picture.

Marcus stood with Anthea in the drawing-room looking up at the rather discoloured patch that was showing where the painting should have been in place.

'When Jennette suggested you might have taken it away to be cleaned, I thought she was being quite sensible for once,' Anthea said.

But the earl shook his head. 'No, I would never have removed it without telling you. It is all rather a puzzle and very worrying. James tells me that there has been no sign of a break-in anywhere and also that there is nothing else missing.'

'Yes, that is right; the three of us looked over the whole house and nothing is out of place. And why should someone want to steal a family portrait in any case?'

'My dear Anthea, the picture may not look anything more than a rather dingy family likeness but it is in fact a Van Dyck when he was at his best and it has always been

184

considered valuable. However, very few people know that which makes it even more of a mystery.' He sat down and said rather irritably to her, 'Do sit down with me and let us think. I really do not know what to do for the best.'

'Do you think we should get the parish constable?'

Marcus shook his head. 'No, he only deals with petty local crimes. I think the best thing I can do is to go and see Sir James Lastingham, the magistrate, first thing tomorrow morning and ask his advice. He lives at Rawcliffe so it is not far to go. In the meantime, I think we had better try and put it out of our minds; it is likely that Sir James might suggest we go to the art dealers in York to see if anyone has tried to sell the picture. I could do that tomorrow, too.' He looked at her. 'It is not possible that someone in the house could have hidden it just to annoy us, is it?'

Anthea frowned. 'What a thing to say, Marcus. I know that Jennette holds it against you that you would not hear of her being wed to Merrick, but I honestly don't think she has the wit to think of anything like that.'

'That is not very complimentary to my ward, but I think I agree with you,' he said drily. 'Come along, come over the house with me again and we will have one more look to make sure nothing else is missing. There are several pieces of Worcester porcelain which are valuable. I would like to check for myself.'

Anthea felt a sense of unease for the rest of the day and learned from the earl just before she retired to her bedroom that he thought Jennette seemed quieter than usual at dinner, seemingly concerned about the loss of the picture. But Miss Craddock had never stopped her prattling and he thought he should go mad before the meal had finished.

The following morning, Merrick arrived without Phoebe and before the usual time for their ride all together. Jennette ran back upstairs for something she said she had forgotten and while she was gone, Anthea asked Merrick if he had any knowledge of the whereabouts of the missing picture. He said he was sorry to hear it was missing and hoped that they had not been burgled.

Jennette appeared then, slightly flushed, and Anthea saw them go off happily together. She waved them off and went for her usual interview with the earl.

'I won't keep you today, Anthea,' he said. 'Have you seen either Merrick or Phoebe this morning?'

'Merrick came on his own for Jennette and they've just ridden off, but he knows nothing of the painting,' she replied.

'Very well, I will ride over to see Sir James, expect me back at about noon.'

But before noon came, Anthea was facing a crisis at Felbeck Abbey. It had started when Jennette did not return from her ride and she imagined some accident to the girl. Then, some thirty minutes later, she was confronted with an anxious and tearful Phoebe who jumped off her horse and came running into the house.

'Mrs Davenport, please tell me if Jennette has come home. Please tell me she is safely here.'

CHAPTER TEN

Anthea drew the distressed Phoebe into the drawing-room only to find that an agitated Miss Craddock was not only sitting there but had heard Phoebe's words in the entrance hall.

'Oh my goodness me, has Jennette met with an accident?' cried Miss Craddock. 'Do tell us what has happened, Phoebe dear. I hope it is not bad news because I think it would overset my nerves and they are already frayed with the business of the picture. It has been bad enough waiting for all this time for Jennette to return from her ride without having bad news to add to my anxiety . . .'

Anthea took one look at Phoebe's troubled face and took matters into her own hands. 'Has Jennette suffered an accident?' she asked quietly.

Phoebe shook her head. 'No, I am sure she is all right but . . .'

'Wait, Phoebe,' said Anthea and she turned back to Miss Craddock. 'Phoebe assures me that Jennette is quite unharmed, you have no need to worry. I will get James to bring you a glass of ratafia and I will speak to Phoebe on her own in my sitting-room. I do not wish to cause you any upset, Miss Craddock. Let me find out what has happened and when Phoebe is gone, I will come and tell you what she has said.'

'Yes, I am sure that is the best for even the sight of Phoebe's tears causes me great apprehension. I will trust you to do what is right, Mrs Davenport.'

Anthea took Phoebe by the arm and led her out of the drawing-room. 'Come into my sitting-room, Phoebe. I will get you a drink for I can see that you have had an upset; then you can tell me the whole.'

Although it was late morning, Anthea had a tray of tea sent in and Phoebe seemed thankful to sip the hot drink.

'Now Phoebe, you will have realized that Jennette is not here and that we have been in a worry about her as she and Merrick set off for their ride quite early this morning. Tell me what you know right from the beginning. Do not leave anything out and don't worry if it is a long story.'

Phoebe had always been a straightforward, honest girl and she took time to gather her thoughts before speaking.

'First thing this morning,' she said in a quiet and composed manner, 'Merrick was in a fidget about something but I could not tell what it was. He went to York unexpectedly yesterday and I thought it must be something to do with that. Then he said to me that he would come over to Felbeck Abbey to fetch Jennette early as he wanted to see her privately—I guessed that it was something to do with the earl not giving him permission to speak to Jennette. He said that they would meet me at Home Wood at about eleven o'clock and I thought it was reasonable and nice of them not to leave me out . . . I am sorry if I am going into too much detail, Mrs Davenport.'

Anthea shook her head. 'No, Phoebe, you are doing very well. I want to know every little thing however trivial, certainly if you think it is important.

'I set out for Home Wood on Sherpa in good time but when I got there, I found no sign of Merrick and Jennette. I waited and waited and I went into the wood to see if they were there though I could not see any sign of their horses. I rode all round the wood for fear I had mistaken the meeting-place but they weren't anywhere. I didn't know exactly how long I was there but I realized later that it was nearly an hour. In the end, I rode back to Downes Hall thinking I must have misunderstood what Merrick had told me.' She paused as though she was trying to think of the best way of telling the next part.

'Go on,' said Anthea gently, but she was beginning to feel fearful.

'My Aunt and Uncle Downes had not seen Merrick since first thing this morning but they did not seem worried. But I was, Mrs Davenport, I was suspicious and I will tell you why in a moment. I went out to the stables—and now I will go slowly for this is the important part. In the stables, I found Tessa and Merrick's horse so I went in search of one of the stable boys to ask if he knew where Miss Jennette and Mr Merrick were . . .

Phoebe took a breath and then went headlong into her story. 'Oh yes, he said, they came home in a rush, handed over their horses to him and told him to have the curricle ready in five minutes which he did. Then, he said, Miss Jennette came back with a band-box and Mr Merrick handed her up into the curricle. Mr Merrick, he had a travelling case, too, and he got up and they drove off at a tearing pace and both of them laughing and giggling as though it was a first-rate joke.'

Phoebe stopped speaking and looked at Anthea. 'That's all, Mrs Davenport, I came straight over here to see if Jennette had returned and of course, she hasn't and . . . oh, Mrs Davenport, I am afraid they must have eloped.'

Anthea got up then and walked about the

small room. Surely Jennette wouldn't have been so foolish? Eloped to Gretna Green with Merrick Downes because the earl had refused to allow them to marry? I know she is a silly girl, she said to herself, and that she imagined herself to be in love with Merrick, but I cannot believe she would be so foolhardy.

She turned back to Phoebe who was more composed now that she had told her story. 'You said you would tell me why you were suspicious, Phoebe.'

The young girl nodded. 'It was really one or two things which seemed to add together and it started after the earl had said he would not allow them to marry. They didn't know it but it showed. I could tell they were excited about something. At the race meeting, if you remember, they went off to the wood and when Jennette returned, I knew something had happened. Then she asked me, quite playfully, if I would elope with the person I loved and I'm afraid I didn't take her seriously.'

'What did you reply?'

Phoebe looked rueful. 'I said that I probably would if we loved each other enough.'

'Oh, Phoebe, but you didn't really mean it?'

'No, I didn't, I only said it in fun and I regret it now,' Phoebe said soberly.

'Was there anything else?'

'Yes, it was when we were riding on the sands at Scarborough. Jennette and Merrick had a race and they were ahead of me and they didn't think I was able to hear what they were saying. But as I caught them up I heard Merrick say ". . . as far as Wetherby and then it will be the stage". Then they saw I was coming and they didn't say anything else but there was a scheming look about them. I didn't think anything of it at the time because we were near the Spaw House and I wanted to try the waters, but no one else wanted to so we didn't go in.'

Anthea looked puzzled. 'But I thought Mr Lorimer was with you.'

Phoebe nodded. 'Yes, he was, but he had ridden over to the Spaw House to see what was going on inside. He came back laughing and saying it was full of old ladies and invalids so we galloped straight back along the sands. I really had forgotten about it until I found the curricle missing just now and I came over to tell you. On the way, I kept remembering different things, they seemed to come back to me.'

Anthea was thoughtful. 'Now I come to think of it, Jennette was wearing her very best riding habit this morning, the one she keeps for special occasions; she never wears it just for a morning's ride with you and Merrick. I didn't take a lot of notice because I was talking to Merrick about the missing painting—did you know the family portrait has been stolen? Jennette didn't say a lot as she had to run back upstairs as though she had forgotten something. Then they said goodbye and disappeared round to the stables to get Tessa. It is not good news, Phoebe, and I fear the worst—'

She stopped speaking abruptly as the door of her room was flung open and the Earl of Felbeck stood there not looking very pleased.

'What is all this I hear from my cousin about Jennette not returning from her ride? Has the damned girl had an accident?' He broke off and looked at Phoebe. 'I'm sorry, Phoebe, you see me not in the best of tempers after a useless ride to ask the magistrate about the painting. He is of the opinion that it must have been stolen by someone in the family, if you please. And where is Jennette? Don't tell me the silly chit has run off with Merrick, that is all the news I need.'

If matters had not been so serious, Anthea would have laughed. As it was, she made Marcus sit down and told him to listen to what Phoebe had to say.

Phoebe refused to go over it all again so Anthea told the earl the main points of the story. As she went on speaking, his expression got more and more black and thunderous.

Then he jumped up. 'She's done it to spite me because I refused to let Merrick make an offer for her. I warned her he was after her fortune, but she would not have it and now it looks as though the little fool has played into his hands. If he gets her as far as Gretna Green, I shall be astonished. He simply wants to cause a scandal so that I will let them have my permission to be married and he can secure her fortune. I know the Merricks of this world. Only one thing means anything to them and that is money. Now we are in a fix. Did you say they were talking about Wetherby and the stage, Phoebe? And they went in a curricle? He never would have taken the curricle if it had been Gretna Green he was heading for; he was planning to drive as far as Wetherby and then get the stage from there.'

He went up to Anthea and spoke urgently. 'Go and see if Stephen is back from his rounds; then tell Jed I want the curricle immediately, the carriage will be too slow. As it is we'll have to go into York to reach the Wetherby road, but then Merrick will have had to do the same if that is the way he has gone. It's a long shot but I think it is worth it. The stupid girl.'

He went off swearing and grumbling while Anthea went in search of Stephen; she caught up with him in the stables.

He listened to her news in silence, swore and then looked sad. 'My poor little girl,' he said. 'I'll go and find Marcus. Wish us luck, Anthea.'

*   *   *

Earlier that morning, Jennette had been in a fever of excitement when Merrick had come to fetch her. She had managed to pack her own band-box without her maid seeing and had slipped out of the house before breakfast to hide it by the front gates where Merrick had said he would pick it up later.

She chose to wear her latest and most fashionable riding dress for she knew she must be a credit to Merrick and she was relieved that Mrs Davenport had been so concerned at asking Merrick about the painting that her smartness had not been noticed. As they rode from the house, she didn't say anything to Merrick. He had already told her of his plans and he seemed preoccupied.

So she didn't speak until he had picked up her band-box and they were on the way to Downes Hall. She was not only excited, she was nervous and felt she must say something.

'What have you told Phoebe?' she asked him.

'I've told her to meet us at Home Wood at eleven o'clock, that will keep her out of the way until we are safely off.'

'Is it all arranged, Merrick?'

'Yes,' he said shortly. 'My travelling bag is in the curricle which will be ready for us when we reach Downes Hall. You haven't changed your mind?'

She shook her head. 'No, it's very exciting and I can't believe it's really happening. It seems so easy. I didn't think eloping would be as simple as this.'

'We've got a long way to go yet, Jennette, just do what I tell you and we'll be fine and dandy. Do you still love me?'

'Of course I do. I wouldn't be here if I didn't love you.'

After that they were silent and on reaching Merrick's home, everything went according to plan. The stable boy soon had the curricle ready for them and Merrick threw in Jennette's band-box and handed her up. In a flash, they were driving away from the house—going swiftly towards York and the Wetherby road. Merrick gave a laugh of delight at their success and Jennette could only giggle.

'Why are we going to Wetherby?' Jennette asked.

'Don't ask me too many questions, it is complicated. But you must see that we cannot travel all the way to Gretna Green in a curricle. I will sell it in Wetherby and we will take the stage from there.'

'But I don't think I should travel on the stage.'

'Of course you can, don't be silly; just do as I say and all will be well.'

She sensed that Merrick, for all his laughter as they had left Downes Hall, was feeling some nervousness about the escapade so she stayed quiet for the rest of the journey.

His mood somehow took the edge off her

excitement and while it gave her great pleasure to be sitting up beside Merrick, she was also given the time to ponder on the enormity of what she was doing. Marcus will be furiously angry with me, she was saying to herself as Merrick tooled the horses in and out of the busy York streets before reaching the quieter road to Wetherby. But I think Stephen will be sad. I don't care how Marcus feels for he has brought it on himself; he only had to give his permission and Merrick and I would be betrothed by now and planning our wedding. But Stephen is a different matter. He has been so kind to me and I love him in a certain kind of way which is quite different to how I feel for Merrick.

Lost in her thoughts, she did not see the green fields spinning past, neither did she notice the little villages of Rufforth and Long Marston until she was suddenly aroused by a shout from a more cheerful-sounding Merrick. 'Ten minutes and we will be there, Jennette, haven't we done well?'

'Were you expecting trouble then, Merrick?'

He gave a short laugh. 'I wasn't sure if my father would pursue us, but it looks as though we've got away with it.'

Jennette had not really known what to expect in the small town of Wetherby, but she certainly had not expected to be left sitting in the curricle on her own while Merrick went into a posting-house to secure rooms for them.

But he came back all smiles and handed her down. 'Very obliging man, the landlord, he could even offer us a sitting-room.'

Jennette was greeted effusively by the landlord whose wife showed her upstairs and left her in a small but comfortable sitting-room.

Merrick joined her there and coming to her, took off her riding hat and tilted back her head so that he could kiss her. 'I've been wanting to do that,' he said. 'And, Jennette, I've had to let the landlord think we are man and wife. It would not have seemed proper for you to have been travelling on your own with me.'

If Jennette showed any qualms about this, she did not show it; she was with her Merrick, they loved each other, and in a few days' time, they really would be man and wife.

'That's all right, Merrick, if you could show me my bedroom, I will unpack my band-box. I shall have to manage without a maid.'

She did not notice Merrick's slight hesitation nor his change of tone and manner. 'The bedroom is here, Jennette,' he said and opened a door at the end of the sitting-room.

Jennette picked up her band-box and walked into a large low-ceilinged bedroom which was simply furnished with a wash-stand, a chest of drawers and one very large bed.

Jennette had often been described as a silly girl but she was a true innocent. She looked around her, frowned and then turned to Merrick.

'Why have I got such a large bed? It is big enough for two. And where is your bedroom, Merrick?'

Merrick had laid his plans well and he knew he now had to be at his most cunning. He shut the sitting-room door behind him, stood beside Jennette and put an arm around her. His fingers gently stroked her cheek, his lips nuzzled at her throat just beneath the collar of her riding coat.

'My dearest Jennette, this is my bedroom, too; it is our bedroom. Tonight we will indeed be as man and wife, there is no need for us to wait until we reach Gretna . . .'

Jennette heard his words as though she had been listening to a stranger. Surely this could not be her Merrick? And she turned from silly chit to termagant in the fraction of a second it took to tear herself from his arms and to stand facing him.

'Merrick Downes, I am not yet your wife and it is no use pretending I am. You will go straight to the landlord and demand a separate bedroom for me. You can sleep in that bed if you like but you will sleep in it on your own.'

Merrick thought that cajolery, flattery and love-making would help but he was soon proved wrong. 'You know I love you, Jennette, I cannot wait until you are really mine, you are so beautiful. Let me kiss you to show you how much you mean to me.' And he pulled her into his arms, running his fingers through her curls as he sought her mouth. But he found he was dealing with a different Jennette. She had always responded so willingly and pliantly to his advances that it was hard to believe the strength in her as she pushed him away and he tumbled back on to the bed.

Jennette had never been so angry in her life—no one, not even Merrick—could treat her like this. And before he could rise from the soft covers, she was bending over him and raining blows on his head with her fists.

Seeing his opportunity, Merrick evaded the blows and grabbed her body until she lay on the bed beside him. She cried and screamed at him until he succeeded in rolling over on top of her and silencing her cries with a savage kiss. Jennette thought she was overcome then. She had his weight on top of her and she was breathless.

Use your wits, she managed to think, and she lay still. Sensing victory, Merrick raised his head and looked at the flushed face and the tousled curls of the girl whose fortune he intended to procure.

'Merrick,' she whispered intimately and he had no suspicion of the craftiness of her nature. 'There is no need for this if we have tonight to look forward to.'

He couldn't believe his luck. 'You mean you will stay as my wife?'

'I have no choice, have I? You have already

told the lie to the good landlord and his wife, and as you say, in a few days time we will be in Gretna Green.'

They sat side by side on the bed and looked at each other. 'We are not going to Gretna Green,' he told her.

She stared. Had she heard him aright? 'What are you saying?'

'We can't go to Gretna Green. I have no money,' he said. And he said it casually because he thought he had won her over.

'But we are staying at this inn.'

'I have enough money for that, I stole the picture and pawned it.' Merrick was suddenly confident, not only in his planning but in the fact that he had easily persuaded Jennette into staying the night with him at this inn, and in this bed. He chuckled within himself.

'*You* stole the painting?' Jennette was unbelieving and wondering whatever she was going to hear next.

'Yes, it was easy. I just let myself in when you were all at breakfast and took it and then later in the morning when you and Phoebe were out riding, I went into York and pawned it. *And* I got five guineas for it.'

Jennette was looking at the young man she thought she had loved. It can't be the same person, she said to herself.

'That's what you were doing in York?'

'Yes, that's right. I knew you and Phoebe would be all right together.'

201

'Are you a wicked person, Merrick?'

He smiled and it was rather a lazy, complacent smile. 'Not really wicked, just down on my uppers. I need the money, you see. It was very easy once I met you and found out that you were an heiress. I did like you, I must tell you that,' he added hastily. 'I thought we could be married and my troubles would be at an end. But Marcus spoiled it all.'

Jennette was staring in fascination and, at the same time, with a sense of horror.

'So you thought that if we got to Gretna Green to be wed, you would have access to my fortune,' she said calmly.

'Not quite like that. Had it all planned. Would tell you we'd elope to Gretna but only come as far as Wetherby. Spend the night here as man and wife and you would be disgraced and Marcus would let me marry you straight away to hush up the scandal-mongers.' He could see her breath coming more quickly as her temper rose within her. 'No, don't take a pet. I did love you as much as I'd ever loved anyone and you were pretty enough. I thought we would suit. Better than you and Marcus at any rate. So it's easy, Jennette, you stay the night with me in this nice comfortable bed and Marcus will find out and we can be married. How's that for a good scheme?'

Jennette had indeed let her rage boil up within her as he was speaking but she said nothing. She bent over, picked up her riding hat but did not put it on; then she took hold of her band-box and stood looking at her former love.

'You are despicable, Merrick Downes, in fact you are a traitor to the good name of Downes. Why I did not see through all that charm I cannot imagine. I've been a fool. You'll not get a penny of my fortune, I will make sure of that, and so will Marcus. And I'll have you bound over for a thief for stealing the picture and then abducting me . . . and . . . and holding me against my will and trying to seduce me.' Jennette's voice had risen higher and higher until she was screaming at him. 'And I won't stay in this place a minute longer. You don't know it, but I have money in my reticule and I will take the stage back into York then I can easily hire a chaise to take me home.'

Merrick had stood up and taken her by the arm. 'You cannot travel on the stage by yourself, Jennette.' He still sounded casual enough for he knew the girl was compromised and did not believe that Jennette would ever have the pluck to take any action on her own account.

But she was furiously shaking off his arm and her voice was even angrier. 'You leave me alone. If you say anything more or touch me again, I will tell the landlord to lock you in the room and I will go and fetch the constable to you.'

Merrick looked at the hysterical girl and he knew he had the choice of taking her by force or escaping from the scene. He chose to make his escape. He let Jennette run down the stairs before him, then, while she was talking in some agitation to the landlord, he slipped past her and was round to the stables in a flash. With the five guineas still in his pocket, he was in his curricle and travelling as fast as he could up the Great North Road.

Jennette refused to pay an irate landlord, found out where the stage went from and minutes later, was running up the main street of Wetherby with tears of both rage and pity streaming down her cheeks.

CHAPTER ELEVEN

In the meantime, Marcus was getting the best from his horses as he and Stephen raced off in pursuit of Jennette and Merrick. They said little for Marcus needed all his concentration taking the Wetherby road corners without upsetting his team or his curricle.

But, as they approached the town, Stephen at last put the question which had been bothering him. 'Marcus, we can't be sure of finding them in Wetherby. What will you do?'

Marcus was grim. 'I shall try every posting-house, inn and hostelry and if we don't find them, I shall be both disappointed and angry. So be warned, I am at a pass.'

They called at a small run-down tavern situated near the turn-pike before they had reached the main street of Wetherby. Here Marcus drew a blank, jumped back into the curricle and drove into the town.

The next inn was a posting-house and looked more promising. Marcus hurried inside while Stephen found a boy to attend to the horses. When he followed Marcus, he discovered his cousin to be in heated argument with the landlord, a very stout man with sparse hair which looked as though it had once been red.

And his present temper certainly might have belonged to a red-headed person. Stephen just caught his last words for it looked as though Marcus had only that minute come across the incensed innkeeper.

'. . . a young lady? A young madam, I would say, her being married to the gentleman and looking no more than a schoolroom miss . . . where are they? I don't know, such a performance as I've never witnessed in all my days as the owner of this inn.'

Stephen caught hold of Marcus's arm. 'What is it, Marcus, are they here?'

Marcus was terse. 'Be quiet, I'm trying to get the facts out of this nodcock . . . it sounds as though it might be the pair of them.' He turned back to the landlord. 'Could you try and tell me everything from the moment they arrived and give me a description of the young lady?'

But coherence was impossible from the outraged man. 'Came in here like a lord and ordered my best bedroom and sitting-room for him and his wife and in she trips looking no more than seventeen years of age . . . what colour was her hair? Well, I couldn't see under that riding hat she was wearing but when she ran off after the shenanigans we had upstairs, it was all gold curls tumbling round her shoulders like a doxy . . . and then he appears while I'm having a word with the young miss— she was no wife, that I'm sure of—and he goes off without paying me a penny and such a crying and shrieking coming from the room, I'm sure I've never heard the like. I was going to send the missus up to see if the young lady was all right . . . oh, thank you, sir. Five guineas. I'm sure that's more than enough for the rooms, but I need to be reimbursed for the trouble I've been put to . . . how long ago? Let me think, I tried to catch them but they'd gone without paying me a penny and him up to no good that I'm sure of even if he did have the look of a gentleman bang up to the nines. So I went and told the missus all about it not ten minutes since . . . where did they go? You come along and I'll show you.'

Marcus looked at Stephen. 'It must be them, it looks as though we are too late.'

At the door of the inn, the fat owner of the establishment pointed up the street. 'By the time I'd got out here, there was the young gentleman in his curricle driving up through the place as though there was nothing else on the road and this being the Great North Road, too . . . together? No, they weren't together. He was on his own and she was asking me where the stage went from and went running up the street, still crying she was and carrying her band-box . . .'

But Marcus was on his way up the street and shouting to Stephen as he went, 'Come along, Stephen, she may still be waiting for the stage. I don't suppose there's more than one a day but the little simpleton wouldn't know that.'

As they reached the next posting-house, both of them saw a small figure come down the steps of the inn and stand uncertainly and forlornly on the cobbles.

'There she is, that's Jennette,' shouted Stephen and Marcus had a job to keep up with him as he sprinted ahead.

'Jennette,' called Stephen and when she turned round and saw that it was indeed Marcus and Stephen, tears of joy, mixed with relief and incomprehension, streamed down her face.

'Oh, Stephen,' she cried out. 'How ever did you know I needed you so badly?' And she threw herself into Stephen's arms and clung to him as though she never wanted to let him go, leaving an amused and thankful Marcus looking on helplessly. His eyes met Stephen's over the top of Jennette's head and the look seemed to say 'She's chosen me' on Stephen's part and 'You are welcome to her' from Marcus.

But it was Marcus who took control. 'This looks a better sort of inn, we will leave the curricle at the other place and I will go and bespeak a nuncheon for us here. Then there will have to be some explanations, Jennette.'

Jennette, from the safety of Stephen's arms, raised her head and said, 'Thank you, Marcus.'

Then she looked up at Stephen with a look of confusion and a rare hint of shyness. 'I am so pleased to see you, Stephen, I feel so safe now you are here. However did you know where to look for me? Am I in disgrace?'

He told her of Phoebe's suspicions and with his arm still holding her close, he led her into the inn not knowing what Marcus was going to say to his errant ward.

Some food and some ale seemed to restore their spirits and soon the questions began.

Jennette was both sorrowful and penitent. 'I know I have been foolish and I have behaved very badly,' she told Marcus. 'And I deserve to be punished for running off with Merrick. You would not let us marry so I thought it would be an adventure to go to Gretna Green. Now I know how wrong I have been and how I shouldn't have trusted and loved Merrick as I

208

did. I can't tell you the whole, it is so dreadful, but he wanted to keep me at that inn tonight to cause a scandal—do you know, Marcus, he had even procured a room with only one bed, that was when I knew how wicked he was. It was to get at my money, you know, for he hasn't a penny to fly with . . . oh, Marcus, he stole the family picture and pawned it for five guineas. It was to pay for the inn but he went off without paying a penny—you have settled with the landlord? Oh, thank you. I flew into a temper with him and said I would go back to York on the stage, but when I got here, the only stage for the day had gone. There's not another one until the night mail and I didn't know what I was going to do; when I saw Stephen running up the street it was like a miracle.' She stopped at last—Marcus had thought it better to let her run on—and she grasped Stephen's hand. 'You were like an angel sent from Heaven,' she told him and then added hastily, 'both of you.'

Stephen held Jennette's hand tightly and Marcus looked at the two of them. He felt like laughing at Jennette's woebegone tale and her sudden switch of affection to Stephen, but he knew he had his duty to do.

'Jennette?' he said to her and his tone was low and serious. 'I really do think you should be punished for running off with Merrick, but I have the feeling that your experience at his hands has been punishment enough. Now I must say something that you will not like but it must be made clear however hard it is for you to answer me. Did Merrick succeed in seducing you?'

The colour rushed into Jennette's young face but she spoke emphatically and clearly. 'Oh no, Marcus, I think he wanted to and he did try, but that was when I lost my temper with him because I realized what a wicked person he was.'

Marcus spoke kindly. 'Thank you, Jennette. We have found you and we must be thankful that you have come to no real harm. Yes, you can look at me like that for you know I am going to read you a lecture, but I will let you continue to hold on to Stephen's hand.'

Jennette looked shy and tried to drag her hand away but Stephen was not going to let go of it. 'I am sorry for everything, Marcus. Have I disgraced you as well as myself?'

He shook his head. 'No, for no one will ever know that this morning has been nothing more than a trip to Wetherby. Though why anyone should want to go to Wetherby is beyond my comprehension except for it being an important stop on the Great North Road.' He paused. 'Now I want you to listen carefully. You will know now why I would not countenance a union between Merrick and yourself. I will not dwell on the matter, but I must remind you of my own intentions and the promise I made to your father. I had not meant to marry you so soon as I thought you should have a couple of seasons in local society. But now this has all happened and I will hasten my plans for our marriage. Do you understand?'

Jennette had quickly put the unfortunate events of the morning behind her and was once again the little firebrand. 'No, Marcus, it is kind of you but I won't marry you for I don't love you. Oh, I know you promised Papa and you have been very good to me since he died, having me to Felbeck Abbey and everything . . . but I don't love you and I would rather marry Stephen if I marry anyone. You would marry me, wouldn't you, Stephen?'

Marcus looked at his cousin and saw, with astonishment, the expression on Stephen's face. That is how I feel for Anthea, he told himself. He loves the chit and I think it would do, by Jove, I think it would do.

But Stephen was both cautious and level-headed. He got up and pulled Jennette up beside him. 'I am in no mood to talk or think of marriage, Jennette. The most important thing is to get you back to Felbeck Abbey for there are several people who will be worrying about your welfare. I don't know if Marcus's curricle will take the three of us but you are quite little and we will have to sit close.' He looked at Marcus who nodded at him with some thankfulness. 'I think we can walk back to the other hostelry. You will need your

211

hat, Jennette.'

'Yes, Stephen,' said Jennette obediently.

And Marcus followed the pair of them out of the inn with the delighted feeling that an onerous and somewhat reluctant responsibility had been lifted from his shoulders.

*   *   *

After Marcus and Stephen had left so hastily, Anthea invited Phoebe to stay for a nuncheon and the girl accepted gratefully, she had told her aunt and uncle she was visiting at Felbeck Abbey.

But when Phoebe had gone home, Anthea found herself with a fretful Miss Craddock and a lot of time on her hands. She had told Miss Craddock a little of what Phoebe had said, but had embroidered the truth so that the companion had no suspicion of an elopement. Anthea thought somewhat ruefully that if the word had even been mentioned in jest, that she would be left with a case of hysterics and probably a fainting fit.

It occurred to Anthea that Jennette might possibly have left a note for her guardian to the effect that she was eloping with Merrick and rather guiltily, she searched both the earl's study and the library. But no tell-tale missive was to be found and she went up to Jennette's bedroom to have a look there. She was immediately rewarded.

At Jennette's dressing-table, she moved the girl's jewel-box hastily when she caught sight of an edge of white paper showing itself from underneath. But it was no letter. She picked up a tiny scrap of paper with three words scribbled on it.

LADY PECKITTS YARD

'Wherever is Lady Peckitts Yard,' she said out loud to herself and whatever can it mean? Is that where Jennette is to be found? Can it possibly be that they are not on their way to Gretna Green but that this is the address of the place where they will be staying? Even more questions ran through her mind as she went downstairs in a puzzle to seek out James, the footman. If it is a local place, then James will know, she was saying to herself.

James was found in what had at one time been the butler's pantry and he took the piece of paper from Anthea.

He frowned as he read it. 'I've never been there, Mrs Davenport, but I believe it is a small street in the centre of York. It is in the area of the market in Pavement and I think you would find it was small shops, linen-drapers and the like.'

'Thank you, James.' Anthea said no more and went off in a quandary. The piece of paper was put there by Jennette for a special reason, she thought, I think I will take a trip into York

213

and make a few enquiries. There is no knowing that the dash to Wetherby by Marcus and Stephen may have been quite fruitless as well as frustrating if they have not found the pair of them.

She found a light pelisse of pale green with matching bonnet, put the piece of paper in her reticule and went in search of Samuel-Coachman.

He was idle in the earl's absence and quite willing to take the housekeeper on a shopping trip to York.

She left him at the Black Swan in Coney Street, telling him she was going in the direction of Pavement and that she would be back within the hour. She found him quite willing to sit and chat with the other coachmen similarly left at the hostelry.

Anthea had become acquainted with most of the streets in the centre of the city as she had sometimes gone with Sarah on shopping expeditions. She knew that the market in Pavement was where Sarah bought her fish.

So from Coney Street, she hurried round the corner into High Ousegate and on asking for Lady Peckitts Yard was directed to the Golden Fleece, one of the coaching-inns of the city. The courtyard lay behind the inn, she was told.

She found it without difficulty but with continued bewilderment. In the courtyard that was indeed Lady Peckitts Yard, she found overhanging, timber-framed houses and a few shops. She looked around her at a complete loss. Whatever would Merrick and Jennette be doing in such a place? Surely he had not found a lodging and taken Jennette to it to set her up as his mistress? No, she could not believe that even the rakish Merrick would do such a thing. What would be the advantage except perhaps to extract some of Jennette's money from her guardian?

I am at a standstill, she had to admit to herself, but I am here and I will walk round the yard and see if any enlightment comes. She did find a small linen-drapers, but no, she was politely told, they did not know of a Miss Goodison or a Mr Downes.

The next shop to it, Anthea thought, was a watchmaker's or even a silversmith's; its windows were clean and through the small panes, she could see several gentlemen's silver watches together with some other pieces of jewellery. But alongside these items were some embroidered waistcoats and a few bonnets.

Puzzled, she looked closer. On the counter at the back of the shop, she could see piles of various garments and objects which seemed to have no place in any shop. Then, looking up, she realized that she was standing outside a pawnbroker's. A man was standing behind the counter looking at her and, as she hastily moved on, her eye was caught by a picture hanging on the wall behind his head.

Anthea stood rooted to the spot.

She could not believe it. For it was the very portrait of the Lorimer family stolen from Felbeck Abbey the day before. Before she had time to catch her breath, let alone start to think, the door of the shop was opened and the man from behind the counter was speaking to her.

'Can I help you, ma'am, do not be afraid to enter if there is any article you wish to deposit with me.'

And without any sense of having moved, Anthea found herself in the most amazing room she had ever been in. So this was a pawnbroker's?

There were clothes everywhere and not all of them new or even clean, ball-gowns jostled with baby clothes, bonnets with boots; boxes of tools from various crafts were placed beside crates of vases and cups and other crockery. She saw a tarnished brass fender and several swords, a great many clocks and even a pair of stays: whatever might fetch a few pence to its owner had been brought to the pawnbroker.

But fascinated though she was, Anthea could not take her eyes from the picture which was still in the gold frame she had cleaned so carefully.

'The portrait,' she stammererd.

'Yes, ma'am, quite valuable I think if it is a Van Dyck as I believe to be the case. Brought in only yesterday, have you the ticket?'

Anthea floundered. What did she know of pawnbrokers? Yes, you took in an article in exchange for money and were given a ticket to claim it back. Is that what the piece of paper was? She put her hand in her reticule, pulled out the piece of paper and handed it to the man who was regarding her rather oddly. He seemed quite respectable, she thought, tall and thin and neatly dressed and so far he had been very polite.

'Is this it?' she asked.

He looked at the scrap of paper and flung it down scornfully. 'This is simply my address, you can see that. What do you want with the picture? Five guineas I gave for that, nearly as much as a whole day's takings.'

Anthea decided to risk everything. 'I am the housekeeper to the Earl of Felbeck of Felbeck Abbey. That is a portrait of his ancestors of the Lorimer family; it was stolen from the house yesterday and I wish to claim it back.'

'Not without no ticket, you don't. And I don't believe you. Anyone can see you're a lady and no housekeeper and it was a young blade as brought it in. Five guineas I gave him.' He repeated the amount as though it was a preposterous sum to him. 'And if he did steal it, he is likely to get a hefty fine, and if he can't pay that then it's fourteen days' hard labour or a public whipping.'

'I don't know who stole it,' Anthea replied though by now she had a good idea that

217

Merrick himself had been the thief. 'But I want it back. His Lordship has been to see Sir James Lastingham, the magistrate, and you will be in trouble for receiving stolen goods if you are not careful. So please give me the picture and we'll say no more.'

She was not quite sure of her facts here, but at the sound of the magistrate's name, the pawnbroker became both agitated and threatening. 'Don't you threaten me, miss, there's something havey-cavey going on and I'm fetching the constable.'

'All right then, fetch the constable. I will wait here until I get the picture back.'

If Anthea had been able to read his expression, the next moves would never have taken place for he was suddenly more than polite, almost grovelling.

'If you please, ma'am. You can sit in my room at the back comfortable while I am gone, I won't be away more than ten minutes.'

'Very well,' she said, glad to sit down though she would have been quite content to have been left in this shop with its fascinating collection of odd items.

She was shown into a very small room, not a lot bigger than a large cupboard, but it was neat and clean, furnished with just a table and a chair and rather strangely, a bookcase full of old leather-backed tomes which the pawnbroker had obviously been left with but had not wanted to sell with his other uncollected items.

'I will wait,' she said as she sat down and afterwards knew herself to be foolishly innocent and unsuspecting. For as the pawn-broker went back into the shop, she heard him turn a key and when she jumped up and tried the door, she knew she was locked in. She banged on the door but no sound came from the other side and she assumed he had left to fetch the constable.

Oh my goodness, what now? she said to herself as she sat at the table. I'll just have to wait for the constable and hope he can sort it out.

But the constable did not come and in the time that she sat there, Anthea had many bitter thoughts. She reasoned that the pawnbroker would not fetch the constable until he had finished business and that could be several hours away. And there was Samuel-Coachman waiting for her at the Black Swan with no idea where she had gone.

Merrick must have stolen the picture, was her next thought; he needed the money badly and every little would have helped. Five guineas goes a long way. And whether he marries Jennette or not, he will be sure of either her fortune or Marcus funding him to hush up the scandal.

She heard people come and go in the shop. Mostly women's voices and she thought a few children. She banged on the door but the pawnbroker took no heed; she sat with her head in her hands beginning to despair, but determined not to give way to tears. The man could not keep her there for ever. She even looked at the window to see if she could climb out, but it was small and high up and looked permanently sealed. No fresh air has ever entered this room, she thought, I suppose I should be thankful that it's clean and that I've got somewhere to sit.

She set herself thinking of Marcus and Stephen, wondering if they had managed to catch up with Merrick and Jennette. She wondered what Samuel-Coachman would do and how soon he would go back to Felbeck Abbey. Then she gave herself a crumb of comfort as she remembered that she had asked James where Lady Peckitts Yard was and he had seen the piece of paper.

Anthea would have been happier if she had been able to see all the activity at Felbeck Abbey.

*   *   *

The first event was the arrival of Marcus, Stephen and Jennette.

Marcus handed Jennette down and told her to run and tell Miss Craddock that she had been on a trip to Wetherby with Merrick; they had had a quarrel and Marcus had found her and brought her home. 'It sounds a tall story,' he said, 'but no word of an elopement or we'll have the vapours. I will go and tell Mrs Davenport and send a message to Downes Hall. I can ride over tomorrow and tell them the whole.'

But Marcus could not find Anthea. That was his first mystery, the second being that his carriage and Samuel-Coachman were both missing. So he went in search of the good James.

'James, did Mrs Davenport say she was going to be out?'

'Yes, My Lord, I believe she asked Samuel to take her in the carriage to York; something about a linen-drapers, I believe.' Marcus frowned, that did not sound like Anthea. 'She said nothing more?'

'Oh yes, she asked me if I knew where Lady Peckitts Yard was, she had the name written down on a piece of paper.'

'Lady Peckitts Yard?' said the earl, still frowning. 'What the devil would she want there? Do you know the place, James?'

'It's a little yard off Pavement, My Lord. Some houses and a few shops, I believe, and a pawnbroker's.'

'A pawnbroker's?' More mystery, Marcus thought. 'And you think Mrs Davenport might have gone there?'

'I don't know, My Lord.'

Marcus went off in a frenzy of frustration. Would this day never end? The stolen portrait and the magistrate; Jennette's elopement; and now Anthea's disappearance.

It was no more than a few minutes later that the carriage returned and Samuel was there asking to see his master.

Marcus went out to the stables where he found Samuel handing the carriage over to Jed.

'No, don't put it away,' he barked. 'I may need it. Samuel, where is Mrs Davenport?'

Samuel was usually a cheery countryman but that day, his face looked drawn and miserable.

'I've lost her, My Lord, I'm that worried.'

'You've lost her?' the earl thundered. 'How the deuce can you lose someone in York?'

'It's easy, My Lord. You see, she didn't tell me quite where she was going except it was in the direction of Pavement. Well, I hunted everywhere when she didn't return within the hour as she said she would; all round the market, up by that church, but no sign of her anywhere. I even enquired at the Black Swan thinking she might have needed some refreshment but no one knew of her, My Lord. So in the end, I thought it best to come straight back and tell you.'

'You did right, Samuel—' Marcus stopped with a sudden thought. 'Samuel, tell Jed to put the horses to the curricle again.'

'But they'm beat, My Lord. Jed says you must have driven them very hard wherever you went.'

'Well, for God's sake, find two others.'

And the earl stormed off. In search of Jennette, this time. He found the girl talking to Miss Craddock in the drawing-room; at least she's calmed the old biddy down, he thought irreverently.

'Jennette, come into the library. I want to ask you something.' His tone was fierce and Jennette looked frightened. 'No, I am not going to read you a scold, it is information I am looking for and I think you might be able to help.'

They sat in the library and at first, Marcus was quietly thoughtful. Certain things seemed to be connecting themselves in his mind and they might explain Anthea's disappearance.

The stolen portrait? The pawnbroker? Lady Peckitts Yard? Was it possible or was he being a fool about his missing love?

'Jennette, listen carefully. Does the name Lady Peckitts Yard mean anything to you?'

She hesitated only for a second. 'Yes,' she replied. 'It was written on a piece of paper that Merrick gave me this morning.'

'Before you left with him?'

'Yes, he gave it to me. It was folded up and he said to go and put it somewhere safe on my dressing-table. So I ran upstairs and put it under my jewel-box, but I looked at it first. All it said was Lady Peckitts Yard and I couldn't understand so I forgot all about it. Why?'

Marcus went slowly. 'It was under the jewel-box . . .' He jumped up. 'Run and see if it is there now, Jennette, quickly.'

She took to her heels and was back in minutes, shaking her head. 'No, it's gone, Marcus.'

'Now listen again. Did Merrick mention the stolen painting to you?'

He watched her face which was in a puzzle. 'But I told you, Marcus. He stole it and took it to a pawnbroker's and got five guineas for it . . . Marcus, where are you going?'

'Stay here, Jennette, I am going to Lady Peckitts Yard and I think I am going to find Anthea.'

She looked bewildered. 'Isn't Mrs Davenport here? I thought I hadn't seen her.'

'No, she's missing and I think that Lady Peckitts Yard is the clue. Thank you, Jennette. Oh, and will you go and tell Stephen that I have gone to York.'

He rushed from the room and Jennette thought he had a look of triumph about him.

She went in search of Stephen and found him in the kitchen talking to Sarah about Mrs Davenport's disappearance; she gave him Marcus's message and told him about the picture.

Stephen smiled at her. 'So one mystery solved and now we have another, but I am sure Marcus will find Anthea.' He touched her arm. 'Jennette, come into my office, I want to talk to you. This seems to be a crazy day.'

In his office, Stephen turned to her and held out his arms. Jennette went willingly into them and he laid his cheek against her curls. 'This is where I want you to be,' he told her. 'You need protecting and I want to protect you. Will you let me?'

She looked up at him with a smile which was at the same time, shy and crestfallen. 'What are you saying, Stephen?'

'I am asking you to do me the honour of becoming my wife. I know that I should ask Marcus first but I've a feeling he understands.'

'Stephen, I cannot be your wife, I have been too wicked. I am expecting to be punished for running off with Merrick, you know.'

He bent down and gently touched her lips with his and what began as a polite and caring kiss became more intense as they each became aware of a love and need for each other.

'Stephen,' Jennette breathed.

'Will that do for a punishment?' he asked in a voice full of fun.

'Don't tease me, Stephen, I am disgraced and you know it.'

'My love, listen carefully to me. You ran off with Merrick and that was very wrong, but you would not let him have his way with you. You managed to get away from him and we got there in time, didn't we?'

'Oh, Stephen, when I saw you I couldn't

believe it. I seemed to go from Hell to Heaven in a single second. But what about Marcus? He is not pleased with me,' she said soulfully.

'I think the worst thing Marcus could do in the way of punishment is to insist that you marry him and I don't think he is going to do that somehow.'

'How do you know?' she asked.

'Two things; one I am sure of and one I am guessing.'

'You are teasing me again.'

'I am sure he knows I love you and you told him yourself that you would rather marry me than marry him, you little minx. And the other is that I think that Marcus and Anthea are made for each other and I earnestly hope that he will find her in York and that they will come together.'

Jennette laughed then. 'It sounds like a fairy-story, happy ever after,' she told him.

'So what is your reply to my question?'

'Which question?'

'Will you marry me? I should have told you that I love you and have done from the moment I first saw you; but of course, I had no hopes because of Marcus's position.' He kissed her again persuasively as though he was trying to urge the right answer from her lips.

'Oh, Stephen,' Jennette sighed. 'I do love you, I know it now. I loved you in a way from the start for I could always put my trust in you; I felt safe. It wasn't like the love I thought I

226

felt for Merrick; I suppose I was flattered and dazzled. I can see now that it was a foolish passion that was never meant to last. Will you forgive me for behaving as I did and running off with him? I must have been in a state of muddle-headed madness for as soon as I realized what a terrible person he was, the love just seemed to vanish as though it had never been.'

'I will forgive you if you say yes to my question.'

'Which question?'

He groaned. 'Can I really love you, foolish creature? I've asked you three times to marry me and this is your last chance.'

'If Marcus says I may then I would like to marry you, Stephen. The answer to your question is yes please.'

'Oh, Jennette, I am sure we will be happy. You won't mind if I continue steward to Marcus? He has a house in the grounds all ready for me; it was the dower house at one time but had fallen into disrepair. Since Marcus came back to Felbeck Abbey, he has been renovating it. I think you will like it and I think Marcus will like having you near even if he is no longer your guardian.'

'Stephen, are you marrying me for my money?' she suddenly shot at him.

He laughed heartily. 'No, you young hussy, I am not. I have a competence of my own. I do not need to work as steward at all but I started by helping Marcus out and now I love it.'

Jennette reached up and kissed his cheek happily. 'We will tell him when he returns, I hope he will be pleased. And I hope he finds Mrs Davenport, too.'

Stephen looked puzzled. 'Sarah was just telling me that Anthea is missing. Do you know why Marcus has gone to York to look for her? Come and sit with me and tell me all about it.'

CHAPTER TWELVE

In the time that it had taken Stephen to persuade Jennette to marry him, Marcus had reached York, left the curricle at the Black Swan and was striding down Pavement looking for Lady Peckitts Yard. It was by now well into the afternoon, the day was warm and there was a smell of fish and rotting vegetables in the market. He carefully picked his way through and found Lady Peckitts Yard hidden behind the Golden Fleece.

It took him only seconds to find the pawnbroker's but he did not go straight in; just as Anthea had done, he looked at the extra-ordinary collection of objects which had been pawned and then felt himself stiffen as his eye caught sight of his family portrait.

So it all fits together, he thought with

satisfaction. Merrick took the picture from its place and pawned it, but must have had a feeling of guilt as he made Jennette put the pawnbroker's address where it would be found easily.

But that is all very well, he was thinking, here is the pawnbroker, here is the picture, but where is Anthea? She obviously did not succeed in redeeming the picture and yet we know she set out for the place.

He went in, his usual imposing self if somewhat travel weary; the cut of his coat proclaimed the gentleman and his air and his presence immediately impressed itself upon the pawnbroker. 'My Lord . . .' the tradesman started to say.

'Yes, I am "My Lord",' replied Marcus loftily. 'Marcus Lorimer, Earl of Felbeck. You have the portrait of my family hanging on your wall and I would be glad to have it back.'

'Yes, My Lord, but have you the ticket . . .?' But the pawnbroker's voice was drowned by a hammering on the door at the back of the shop and then the scream of a voice.

'Marcus, Marcus!'

For Anthea, half drowsing in the chair of the tiny room, had heard the unmistakable voice of her love announcing who he was. It was unbelievable that he had found her, but she jumped up, banged on the door and shouted his name as loudly as she could.

In the shop, Marcus did not move, even

though his heart thumped when he knew that indeed Anthea was here.

'I believe you have my housekeeper locked in,' he said smoothly to the now flustered pawnbroker.

'Yes, My Lord, that's what she said but how was I to know? She didn't have the ticket and she said the picture had been stolen. I was going to fetch the constable as soon as I shut up shop.'

'Kindly unlock the door,' interrupted Marcus evenly.

The pawnbroker took the key from his pocket, unlocked the door and in seconds, Anthea was in Marcus's arms. He held her tightly and let her cry.

'A fine way for a lord to behave with his housekeeper,' said the pawnbroker.

'Enough of your insolence, man; give me the picture and say no more or I will be getting the law to you for the wrongful imprisonment of a young lady.'

Tickets forgotten and with no mention of money, the pawn-broker hastily lifted the picture down and gave it to the earl, glad to get rid of his troublesome clients.

Marcus paused and tilted Anthea's face to his. 'You are not harmed, my love?'

Anthea ignored the endearment and shook her head. 'No, it was just the waiting. I knew it would be all right once the constable came, but I didn't expect you to come first, Marcus. I

230

couldn't believe it when I heard your voice.' She stopped to feel the touch of his lips on hers and then smiled. 'I am very hungry, Marcus.'

The pawnbroker watched them go and shook his head ruefully. Who could argue with an earl and what was an earl doing kissing his housekeeper? And I've lost five guineas over that one; it's a sorry business. Then his thoughts were interrupted by the sudden return of the earl.

'I believe you to be an honest man even if you did lock up my housekeeper. She insists that you should have the five guineas you paid out for the picture and you did let us have it without the ticket, after all.'

The pawnbroker beamed. 'Thank you, My Lord.' And he watched the tall gentleman return to the courtyard and put his arms round the young lady who was laughing up at him. 'Curst rum touch,' he said to himself.

'Mrs Davenport,' the earl was saying as they walked through the crowded city streets, 'you know that I am not best pleased with you.'

Anthea, knowing she had shown feelings she had not wished to be revealed, was not sure how to take his words.

'My Lord, my only wish, my only thought when I saw the address was to try and find Jennette. But you must tell me at once, did you and Stephen find her safely in Wetherby? Have you brought her home again?'

'Yes, to both of those questions,' he replied. 'I will tell you all about it later. I left Jennette with Stephen and came chasing after you. I've never known such a day. Please go on and tell me why you came here.'

Anthea continued. 'When I saw the address, I imagined that Merrick must have taken Jennette there though I admit to being puzzled when James told me what kind of place it was. Needless to say, I was even more puzzled when I saw the courtyard. I even thought that Merrick must have procured lodgings for them.'

'You did think the worst of him, did you not?' he said and realizing that they had reached the Black Swan, he had to decide on his next course of action. He was tempted to drive back to Felbeck Abbey straight away to find out if he was free of his pledge to his ward, but he knew that the young lady gladly holding on to his arm was in need of food. 'We are at the Black Swan, Anthea, shall I order a dinner for us? I will see if I can procure a private room.'

She nodded thankfully. 'Yes, please, My Lord, I would like that more than anything. There are so many things I must ask you before we return to Felbeck Abbey.'

They were served a good plain dinner of Julienne soup and trout with Dutch sauce, followed by a second course of saddle of mutton and finishing with gooseberry tart and cream. Anthea ate in silence and with some appreciation; she was sitting opposite the earl at a small table which was laid out in a high-ceilinged, sitting-room of some comfort.

Afterwards they sat side by side on the ottoman and Anthea smiled her thanks.

'I feel restored,' she told him.

He laughed then. 'I did not know that a mere housekeeper could eat so heartily, but I must say that it did me good to see you recovering from your experience. You did bring it upon yourself, Mrs Davenport.'

'My Lord, it was all very well for you and Stephen. You sprang into action and went chasing off after Jennette, the naughty girl. I was left trying to convince Miss Craddock that nothing dreadful had happened and telling all sorts of untruths to avoid having a swooning chaperon on my hands!'

'But why on earth did you think that Merrick might have taken Jennette to Lady Peckitts Yard when we were sure they were on their way to Gretna Green?' he asked her.

Her brow wrinkled in a frown and he was tempted to put out a finger and smooth the lines away; but he must be careful of his feelings until he knew with certainty of the fate of Stephen and Jennette.

'It does seem silly now,' she replied, 'I must admit to it. But I was in a fret to do something and not just sit and wait with Miss Craddock until you returned with news.'

'So when you got to York and saw the picture in the pawnbroker's, you marched in and demanded it back! That is like you and look at the trouble it got you into. Did you know it was Merrick who had stolen it in the first place and then pawned it?'

'I didn't know, but I guessed from the pawnbroker's description. He needed the money, didn't he?'

'Yes, it has been money and his attempt to secure Jennette's fortune that have been behind his actions and behaviour over the last weeks and months.' He told her then of how they had found Jennette and of Merrick's evil intention.

'Oh, poor Jennette, she trusted him so innocently and it must have come as a dreadful shock to her to find out what his true character was. At least she managed to run away and you found her in good time.'

'It was some luck and some good judgement and a lot of help from the sensible Phoebe. And I must tell you for I think it will amuse you, that when Stephen and I caught up with Jennette, she ignored me completely and threw herself straight into Stephen's arms.'

Anthea was able to laugh at last. 'I'm not surprised; she was very much in awe of you and Stephen was kind to her from the start. It is my belief that he loves her.'

He looked at her seriously. She had taken off her pelisse and bonnet and was sitting in one of her plain housekeeper's dresses. But he thought she looked lovely. Hers was not a beauty that needed frills and ornamentation; the straight, russet-brown cotton, high to the neck and with long sleeves would have looked ordinary on most girls, he thought, but it suited Anthea's splendid brown hair and dark eyes. She had a dignity always. He longed to disturb the dignity and arouse the passion that he knew lay hidden beneath her respectable and formal exterior, but the time had not yet come.

'Anthea,' he had to say it. 'I am still bound to Jennette, you know.'

She looked back at him wondering why he had made the remark. 'You mean you would not release her if Stephen wanted to marry her?'

'I don't know. If Stephen doesn't come up to scratch then I feel I must marry the girl even if I have no wish for her as my wife. I have other plans I cannot tell you about at the moment.'

He is telling me to keep my place, she thought, and any happiness she had felt in his presence vanished. She stood up.

'My Lord, I think we can return to Felbeck Abbey now. Thank you for coming to my rescue even though I do not know how it was you managed to find me.'

He stood beside her and put his hands on her arms. She could feel the warmth of his

235

fingers through the cotton dress and it somehow raised a danger signal.

And his fingers slid up her arms to grasp her by the shoulders and to pull her gently closer to him. She did not resist and he spoke quietly. 'I was alarmed that you were missing and determined to find you so I practised a little detection. James told me you had enquired about Lady Peckitts Yard for a start; then I questioned Jennette and she said that Merrick had stolen the picture and pawned it. She also had seen the address of Lady Peckitts Yard written on a piece of paper that Merrick had asked her to leave—when she looked, the paper was missing. And so were Samuel and the carriage! When he arrived upset because he had lost you, all things made sense and I got the curricle and came to York. You know the rest; were you pleased to hear your rescuer?'

She smiled broadly. 'I have never been so relieved in all my life,' she admitted.

'And do I get a kiss for a reward?'

She knew there was fun in his voice but she ignored it. 'I do not think it is the time for kisses, My Lord, even thank you ones.'

'Try.'

So she reached up to touch his cheek with her lips but he deceived her, turning his head swiftly so that it was his lips which met hers. She was lost then. His lips were telling her things she wanted to know but dare not

236

recognize; they sought her desperately and found what they were looking for.

The two of them broke apart and stared at each other and it was Anthea who regained her senses first. 'My Lord, I think you said it was time to return to Felbeck Abbey.'

His voice seemed to come from afar. 'Yes, Mrs Davenport, you are right to remind me. I have to sort out the affairs of my ward, don't I? This may be the last time you see me as a single man, I shall insist on becoming betrothed to Jennette straight away.'

'Yes, My Lord,' Anthea replied bravely, but her heart was broken.

They spoke little on the short journey back from York to Felbeck Abbey, both of them occupied with thoughts they were trying to hide from one another.

The first person Anthea encountered when she entered the house was Miss Craddock, who seemed to have been hovering near the front door.

'Mrs Davenport, there you are. I knew there was no need for all the fuss and for Marcus to rush off as he did for you are a sensible woman and not likely to behave foolishly as Jennette is apt to do—but such excitement. Dear Stephen has made an offer for her and she has accepted. But of course she has to have permission from Marcus, he being her guardian and promised to her himself. But I think Stephen would make her the better husband for he seems to understand her and keeps her from flying into alt. Marcus is too serious for her; I know it is his wish but it would never do. And it means I can go back to my dear sister when Jennette is married. Not that I minded obliging Marcus and coming to chaperon Jennette but I confess it has not been easy. Jennette is a dear child and very capricious. Look how she went off on this silly trip to Wetherby with Merrick and just the two of them which was not the thing. It was a good job she had Marcus to go and seek her out when she did not return and Merrick having a quarrel with her and leaving her on her own at the posting-house. I am sure I am pleased to see Stephen and Jennette so loving after the silly child chasing after Merrick all the winter; she should have known someone like Merrick would never settle. But I rattle on and you will want to go and see Jennette yourself . . . ah, here is Marcus now. I have been telling Mrs Davenport, Marcus, what a relief it will be not to have Jennette on my hands . . . you have not seen her yet? Oh dear me, I am speaking out of turn, please disregard what I have said. And what is that you have? The portrait? Oh, I am so pleased and how wonderful to see it hanging in its rightful place again . . . and you found it in a York dealers just as Sir James thought you might? I don't suppose we will ever know who took it but that doesn't seem to matter now that it is safely back yes, Marcus, of course I will . . .'

And she hurried from the drawing-room and Marcus who had indeed re-hung the picture above the fireplace, took Anthea's arm in an urgent grasp.

'I must see you, but it will have to be this evening. I have an interview with Stephen now and then I must ride over to Downes Hall to tell them the facts of Merrick's disappearance, I fear they will be very upset and worried. Don't disappear again.' He kissed her quickly and hurried from the room.

In fact, both Stephen and Jennette were waiting for Marcus in the library. They had learned of the successful dash to York and the retrieval of the painting and the safe return of Mrs Davenport.

Stephen spoke as soon as Marcus entered the room. He was holding Jennette's hand very tightly for she was nervous, almost frightened of what her guardian was going to say.

'Marcus, I am going to be formal for this is a serious occasion and I am well aware of your commitments on behalf of Jennette. I ask your permission, as her guardian, to allow me to address myself to her and to ask for her hand in marriage. I know she is willing for she has told me she loves me and I think you are aware of the regard and love I have for her. But all that is beside the point if you feel you must keep your promise to Jennette's father and marry her yourself.'

Marcus felt an explosion of joy burst within him and felt like shouting it to the rafters. But Stephen was being so serious and proper, he must hide his inclination to mirth and reply in the same vein.

But he addressed himself soberly to his ward. 'Jennette, I have willingly taken you into my home and would just have willingly made you my wife. So before we say anything else, I will speak formally just as Stephen has done. I offer you my hand in marriage, Jennette, and I must tell you that in view of you capers today, I would feel that I must announce our betrothal immediately. What have you to say?'

Jennette had expected wrath and was aware that she did not deserve her guardian's kind protection so she did her best to speak in a proper manner.

She went up to him and stood on tiptoe to kiss his cheek. 'Marcus, you have done everything my dear father asked of you but we must remember that had he lived, it is not likely that he would have regarded a union between us as being a suitable one. He was a very loving person and he would have respected that the love that Stephen and I have for each other was important to our future happiness. Stephen is no fortune-hunter as I now know Merrick to have been and I believe that in spite of my foolish behaviour over Merrick, it is Stephen I wish to marry. I decline your kind offer, Marcus, and hope you will sanction a betrothal between your cousin and myself.'

Jennette stopped, she knew she had surpassed herself in correct formality and she looked towards Stephen. She saw pride in his eyes. Then she looked at Marcus and received a shock.

For Marcus was smiling and his eyes met hers with a gladness and a delight. He didn't want to marry me, she thought, I needn't have made that long speech. All her notions of propriety flew with the wind.

'You didn't want to marry,' she blurted out.

And she found herself picked up by her guardian, whirled round and then soundly kissed.

'I would have married you, dear girl, but I am glad you have found Stephen and that you will be marrying a Lorimer. Stephen, I wish you every happiness with this troublesome chit and I gladly give you my permission to address her which you seem to have done already, in any case! I have other plans of my own and as soon as I have ridden over to Downes Hall to give the news of Merrick, I shall put them into practice.'

And he was gone and Stephen took Jennette into his arms and kissed her fervently; she wound her arms round his neck so that he would be even closer to her and, as she felt the passion course through her body, she knew it was combined with a strong feeling of belonging which she had never felt before.

'Stephen, why have I been so stupid? You were there all the time, but I thought of no one but Merrick and looked upon you as a kind brother.'

'Sometimes love that grows is the best kind of love, Jennette,' said Stephen wisely.

She looked at him. 'You are right, as always. I can forget about Merrick; I wonder where he is?'

Stephen laughed and laughed at her remark and kissed her again; his fingers ached to feel the whole of her tempting little body but he knew he must wait patiently for his love. 'I expect that Merrick will stay away for a little while,' he replied.

'And what about Marcus? Are you sure about him and Mrs Davenport, she is his housekeeper, you know?'

'My little love, Anthea only became a housekeeper because she was left destitute and had to fend for herself. Good fortune brought her here and I think she walked straight into Marcus's heart. She is most suited to become the next mistress of Felbeck Abbey for her mother was a Haley of Loxley Hall in Cumberland and a most respected family. But apart from all that, I think they love each other even if they don't know it yet. I have seen the look in Marcus's eyes and he never looked at you like that, Jennette.'

'So do you think we might have two

betrothals in one day?' she asked him with a look of pleasure in her eyes.

He smiled happily. 'Let us hope so,' was all that he would say and proceeded to kiss her yet again.

It was a while before they went in search of Miss Craddock and told her the news and they had to endure a lecture on how good Marcus was, but Stephen was one of her favourite cousins and she was happy for him, and Jennette of course.

Then Jennette, having left Stephen to his books, knocked on Anthea's sitting-room door.

'Mrs Davenport, you must be the first to know—after Miss Craddock, that is—Stephen and I have become betrothed. Dear Marcus has given his permission. He said he would have married me out of a sense of duty but he seemed pleased about Stephen and says he has his own plans though I am sure I don't know what they are. He has gone over to Downes Hall for Merrick's poor parents will be in a worry over him not returning, though of course, he may have gone home by now though I doubt it. He is in disgrace, after all. I expect they will blame it all on me, but Marcus will talk nicely to them. I am so excited, Mrs Davenport, I cannot believe it can all have happened in one day. I am sure I shall never sleep . . .'

Anthea was wondering which was the worse,

Miss Craddock or Jennette, but she knew she was being unkind to both of them for Miss Craddock was as well-meaning as Jennette was excitable.

After Jennette had gone and the evening was drawing to a close, Anthea came to the conclusion that the earl had changed his mind about wanting to see her. She felt so restless and on edge that she found a Kashmir shawl for her sholders and walked out to the ruins.

Her feet seemed to take her in that direction without her even thinking about it and she sat on the stones gloomily. The light was fading but the sky was clear and there was a faint golden glow in the north-west where the sun had gone down. There were no shadows that night but the place seemed shadowy; she shivered and wondered if she had been wise to come. The place was brimming with vivid memories of Marcus and she could not stop herself thinking of him.

She knew now that it was not his intention to marry Jennette and the girl had said that he had other plans. It seems that those plans do not involve me, she said to herself rather sadly, for he must have returned from Downes Hall by now, yet he has not sought me out.

I wonder if I am wise to stay at Felbeck Abbey? I do love the place and it is an ideal position for me, but to be near Marcus and not be able to love him? Perhaps having to see him married to a lady of the local society who would bear his children? I must try not to think about it; I am tired now and I will be able to see things more clearly in the morning. I'd better start walking back to the house before it gets really dark. And she got up from the stones and looked around her with sad feelings.

As she did so, she thought she heard the sound of a horse being galloped hard. And then . . .

'Anthea, are you there, damn you? I've looked everywhere for you, this was the last place I could think of.'

And Marcus was before her, jumping down from his horse and slapping the animal to go home.

'He'll go back to the stables, he knows there's food there . . . what in heaven's name are you doing here when it's getting dark?' He didn't wait for a reply but came and stood close to her. 'You look beautiful.'

Anthea snapped back: 'For goodness sake, don't keep saying that, it doesn't mean a thing. You know very well that I am no more than ordinary so why do you keep saying such balderdash?'

She had changed into a light dress for the warm May evening; it was of the softest cotton, pale cream with a brown sash and it clung to her so that the breeze moulded it round her figure. Her shawl was around her arms for she had not needed it to keep her warm. The neck

245

of the dress was high and was fastened by a row of small pearl buttons from the waist to the neck.

Marcus did not reply to her cross retort, but simply put out a hand and started to undo the buttons of her dress.

'What are you doing?' she said sharply, at the same time feeling a shot of desire and longing sweep through her.

She could not believe his next words. And his behaviour and his actions left her speechless.

'I want to see your lovely breasts which have shown me their promise under all your proper morning gowns; I want to lay my head just there and know that I have found peace at last.'

Anthea could not move. She felt his fingers on her bare skin and he gently sat her on the stones and put his head in that same inviting place where buttons had been opened to reveal her tempting body.

'I love you,' he murmured against her, but she did not heed the words.

Her hand reached to his head and her fingers stroked his hair, she felt the tired tension in him subside as he lay so close to her, then he lifted his head towards her and she bent down and put her lips to his. Anthea gave the kiss, she did not say her love but she showed it. And, suddenly, he knew the meaning of her gestures and he gathered her completely in his arms and would not or could not let her go.

'You love me,' he said. 'Say it, Anthea, please say it.'

'I love you, Marcus.'

'And now you know that you are beautiful?'

'For you I will be beautiful,' she whispered.

'My love.'

And the passion rose in them then, kisses and caresses that both wanted to give and receive so desperately. And when they became quiet again and the light had gone, there were more words.

'I can't see you, I can only feel you,' he said.

She smiled though he could not see it. 'It is enough!'

'Anthea, you know I can ask you to marry me now?' he asked her, quietly serious.

'Yes, I do know. Jennette and Stephen told me of their betrothal and I am very pleased for them.'

'They guessed about us, didn't they?'

'I think they knew before we knew it ourselves,' she replied.

'I have always loved you, but I thought I would have to marry that ninnyhammer of a ward of mine.'

'But, Marcus, I was your housekeeper.'

'What did that matter? You were beautiful, I loved you and that was all that meant anything to me. Have I convinced you that you are beautiful?'

She chuckled. 'They say that beauty is in the eye of the beholder!'

'I'll prove it to you,' he said in a threatening voice which was at the same time full of fun.

'No, I want to talk to you.' She caught hold of his hand which was once more straying in the direction of her bodice. 'Tell me how you got on at Downes Hall. Were Merrick's father and mother very upset?'

'Mr Downes was very quiet, but I thought his wife was going to have hysterics. She was unable to believe that a son of hers could behave in such a way. All their other children have married respectably and Merrick is very much the black sheep of the family. Then his father started to blame himself for being too liberal when the boy was in London. He seemed to think that if he hadn't been so generous with his son's allowance then Merrick wouldn't have got into the dandy-set and started gambling and losing so heavily. It gave Merrick a taste for money which he thought he could satisfy by marriage to Jennette. I'm not saying that Jennette didn't encourage him for she did. He was the first young man of fashion she had met and she succumbed to his flattery and his attentions.'

Anthea was thoughtful. 'Jennette knew at the last that it was wrong and that is to her credit; she is fortunate to have found Stephen. Will they live at Felbeck Abbey, Marcus?'

He tightened his hand around hers. 'Would

248

you care if they did?'

'Not exactly, it's just that it would be nice to have you to myself,' she said slowly.

'But you haven't yet told me if you will be my wife.'

She laughed. 'Haven't I shown you?'

'Yes, but I want to hear the words.'

'I would like to marry you, Marcus.'

'But you don't want to share the house with Jennette and Stephen?' he asked in a teasing tone.

'No,' she replied bluntly.

'Bless you for saying it and you don't have to worry. I've been having the old dower house repaired for Stephen and it will be ready by the time they are married.' He got up. 'Let me kiss you once more and then we must walk back to the house. Look, I will do the buttons up so that you will be respectable.'

And his fingers lingered on her soft skin again and she gave a shiver that was of delight and pleasure and not of cold. 'How soon before I can touch the whole of you, Anthea?'

'Marcus, a gentleman does not say that kind of thing to a lady.'

'This gentleman does to this lady. I want you,' he murmured, his lips close to hers.

'Three weeks?' she said wickedly.

'Time to call the banns? Splendid; I think I can wait that long, Anthea, you will be even more beautiful by then!'

'Marcus,' she protested once again and they

exchanged one last, long kiss before returning to the house.

* * *

Their wedding did indeed take place a month later and before that of Stephen and Jennette which was planned for Jennette's nineteenth birthday.

As Anthea had no close relatives nearby, Mr Downes kindly consented to give her away and Jennette and Phoebe were very pretty bridesmaids in pale blue sarsenet trimmed with delicate small white flowers. They also had the same little flowers entwined in their hair.

Anthea looked magnificent if rather shy. As always, Marcus thought her beautiful. She wore a gown of cream velvet with gold ribbons its only ornament, for Anthea chose something plain even for her wedding gown.

They were married in the small church at Skelton. There was a tradition that the little church was built in 1227 with the stones that remained after the building of the south transept of the cathedral in York. The three girls, together with Sarah and Miss Craddock, had the day before placed flowers of cream and gold around the church and it made it a lovely setting for a happy occasion.

Carriages took the bride and groom and the guests back to a wedding breakfast at Felbeck

Abbey. Sarah had surpassed herself—she admitted later that it had been a delight to her—and the food was temptingly laid out in the dining-room.

Later when they were all gathered in the drawing-room for tea, Mrs Downes announced that she had received pleasant news the day before and that she wanted to share it with her friends. She drew from her reticule a sheet of paper and the smile on her face told those assembled that it must be a letter from Merrick. There had been no news of him and this had caused no little anxiety to his parents. She read it aloud for them all to hear.

Dear Father
I know I have brought disgrace upon the family and I am sorry. My main hope, is that no harm came to Jennette and that perhaps she will have married Stephen who I am sure loves her very much. I'm afraid I had to sell the curricle and horses to pay my way by stage-coach to Liverpool. I did not think you would want me home again. There was also the affair of the stolen painting which I hope has been recovered. I did leave a note to say where it could be found. I have to tell you that I am settled in Liverpool waiting for a passage to Jamaica. I have become acquainted with the owner of a sugar plantation there who is in need of a manager to oversee the sending of sugar to this country. You may not like this but

251

I have little alternative and it will be good honest work of which I am sure you will approve. My passage has been paid for me so I have no need to sail steerage. Please give my loving regards and regrets to my mother and also to Jennette if you see her.

Your son, Merrick

The thought of Merrick working on a sugar plantation was almost too much for the composure of the young people, but as Mr and Mrs Downes both seemed pleased, they did not say anything to express their amusement. Merrick had run away from his petty crime and his shocking behaviour to Jennette, but he was taking on a new responsibilty which might possibly be the making of him.

Marcus and Anthea were to travel in the carriage as far as Richmond that day, then they planned to go across to Cumberland. Marcus would meet Anthea's family and Anthea could retrieve the gowns and personal belongings she had been forced to leave behind.

A tour was made of the Scottish border country and a month later, a proud Marcus handed his wife from the carriage outside Felbeck Abbey.

'Welcome to Felbeck as my wife, Anthea,' he said to her, holding her hands and pulling her close to him.

Anthea's eyes glowed with good humour as

she looked up at him. 'I was quite happy as housekeeper,' she said mischievously.

'You are a rogue, a lovable rogue as I have come to realize these last weeks. I love you for it, Anthea, and I trust you will be happy with me here.' And before she had time to assure him that she would, his lips claimed hers in a welcoming home kiss.